DO SOMETHING THAT MATTERS

21 chapters of life

Yuvaan
books

An Imprint of Unbound Script

Do Something That Matters

Written *by* RJ Kartik

First Edition : January, 2026

ISBN : 978-93-47125-29-4

Publisher : Unbound Script
2/41, Ansari Road
Daryaganj, Delhi-110002
Website : www.unboundscript.com
E-mail : books@unboundscript.com
Phone : 011-35807601

Printer : Yash Printographics
Noida, Uttar Pradesh

Price : ₹ 299/-

DO SOMETHING THAT MATTERS

21 chapters of life

RJ KARTIK

Yuvaan
books

Dedicated to my dearest Dadi Maa,
Papa Ji, Mummy Ji, my life partner Ashvini,
my son Yatharth, and my loving family.

Contents

Preface

When I hosted my first radio show on 1 September 2010, I had just one dream - to take my voice to the world and share my positive thinking with everyone. I wanted to show people how a boy from a small town (Bhawanimandi in Rajasthan) could come to a big city (Jaipur), dream of becoming a radio jockey, and, with complete determination, make his voice reach the world.

In 2017, the CEO of My FM, Mr Harish M. Bhatia, suggested that I take radio stories to social media through videos. I express my heartfelt gratitude to him, because it was through his idea that I received the opportunity to become a voice of hope and reach people across the globe.

When my small stories reached you and you showered them with immense love, I felt that God had chosen me as a medium to spread positivity. Whenever I receive your affectionate messages via email or social media, I realise that I have earned the most precious wealth in life. Your love and blessings are my greatest achievements.

I do not like to call myself a motivational speaker, because I believe that true inspiration already exists within every individual. One only needs to be reminded of one's own inner strength. As a writer, this book is my humble attempt to reconnect you with your power and reassure you that, very soon, you will accomplish something so remarkable that the world will want to become like you.

Along with experiences from my small life, this book also includes stories I heard from my elders and adopted as the essence of my own journey. The first chapter of this book may surprise you, because it is a chapter that usually comes at the end. But that is the uniqueness of this book - it depicts an extraordinary journey from the end to life itself. Through 21 chapters, I have tried to present the journey of life to you. These 21 chapters appear in all our lives; if we understand each one, we can truly enjoy the gift of life.

I request you to feel the energy of every word written in this book. I sincerely hope that your love and blessings, just as always, will continue to accompany me on my journey as an author as well.

On this journey of positivity, I would like to express my heartfelt gratitude to the world-renowned author, Mr Shiv Khera, whose books and messages have inspired all of us. I also extend my sincere thanks to Mr Anand Kumar, the founder of Super 30, whose life journey and unwavering dedication to his students are a great source of inspiration for us all.

For bringing my first book to you, I thank Mr Alind Maheshwari, the CEO of Unbound Script, and the editor, Mr Ashish Mishra, who supported me at every step in making this book reach you.

And yes, as I firmly believe, three elements supported me in writing this book as well - the blessings of my Guru, Paramhans Swami Shri Adgadanand Ji Maharaj; the love and blessings of my family; and my hard work. Because someone has rightly said that there is only one shortcut to success in life, and that is hard work.

Awaiting your love and blessings,
Yours truly, RJ Kartik

1

Death

#Someone said something profound

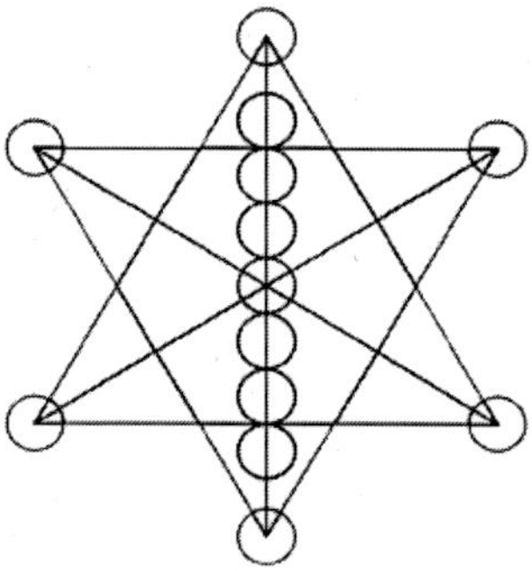

My body is made of dust,
my breaths are borrowed.
What pride can I claim,
when we are all only tenants here?

A wise man once said that the greatest fear in this world is the fear of losing our loved ones. And what everyone is ultimately afraid of is death. Even taking its name makes people uncomfortable; Don't say that word; they whisper. And yet, it is the only thing that makes all of us equal. No matter how much a person achieves in life, everything eventually becomes nothing.

If you're wondering why this is the first chapter of the book, then remember this eternal truth: "The end is the beginning."

Because it is important to understand that even if everything in life ends, it can begin again.

If we believe that there is life after death, then how would you want to live? Your answer will definitely change. Maybe you'll say, "I want to change everything."

So imagine this: Your new birth begins at this very moment.

The rest of the chapters in this book are about that very rebirth: If life gives you another chance, how will you live it? That is why death has been placed at the very beginning.

Have you ever wondered if there were no fear of death, how different this world would be? Evil-minded beings would gain more power, and humans would turn into beasts. It is death that reminds us, "You are not as big as you think you are."

And this fear is what keeps humans, human.

Prince Siddhartha Gautama was born at the foothills of the Himalayas. His father, the king of the Shakya dynasty, had been told by the Brahmins twelve years before his birth, that the child would either become a great emperor or a great sage. To prevent him from becoming a sage, Siddhartha was kept inside the palace walls. He lived in complete luxury, far away from the outside world. Learned teachers educated him inside the palace, and he was trained in warfare within those same walls.

He grew up, got married, and even became a father. But despite living entirely within the palace, the moment arrived that was destined to change everything. One day, when he went out of the palace, he encountered three sights: a sick man, an old man, and a corpse being taken to the cremation ground. His charioteer explained that all beings are subject to illness, old age, and death. This left Siddhartha deeply disturbed.

As he returned, he saw a wandering monk walking peacefully. That moment ignited his desire to seek the answer to human suffering. Without waking his wife and child, he quietly left the palace. At the edge of the forest, he cut off his hair with his own sword, put on simple robes like an ascetic, and began his journey from 'Siddhartha' to 'the Buddha.'

> Someone said something profound:
>
> When your eyes open even before they close, that is true awakening.

Those who understand that life is like slipping sand, that t is passing away every moment, they develop a deeper wisdom. One of our distant relatives had a unique belief. He would cut the cake on his birthday, but never blow the candles. He used to say,

"How can I accept that I have lost another year of my life? Blowing the candle feels like I am moving closer to death." Many people probably feel this at some point. After the birthday celebration, lying in bed, one wonders, "So I'm a year closer to the end."

Life is passing anyway. And if it must pass, let it pass in joy, in peace, and in awareness. That is what it means to truly live.

But we often live with a misunderstanding - I am everything, I am life, I am the one holding my family together.

There was a teacher in a village who had begun to believe the same - that his family survived only because of him. Being a teacher, he also understood his inner self well. When he realized this misconception was turning into ego, he went to an ashram near the forest where a saint lived.

He said, "Guruji, I feel my family depends entirely on me. If I am not there, what will happen to them?"

The saint smiled. "Then go away from the village for two years. When you return, you will see for yourself."

The teacher asked, "But what will you tell my family?"

The saint replied, "I will tell them what I need to tell - that you died in front of my eyes. That a tiger took you away, and I could not save you."

The teacher understood. He left the village immediately. The saint told his family what he had planned. They cried, grieved, and mourned, but slowly, life settled again.

The teacher's son grew up and found a job with the village landlord. His daughter came of age, and the entire village contributed to her grand wedding.

Two years later, when the teacher returned home, he heard laughter from inside. The house was full of joy. His daughter and son-in-law were visiting, and they had a little baby. The teacher walked inside. His family froze for a moment, but he quickly apologized. "I thought you lived because of me... but two years away has shown me that this world is run by someone far greater than any of us."

Often we think, "What will happen if I'm not here?". But this world has existed forever, and it will continue to. Those who left before us must have thought the same - that everything runs because of them. This fear of death is what keeps us rooted in our values.

In the Ramcharitmanas, when Lord Shri Ram asked the ocean god for a path and received no answer, He lifted His bow. At that moment, Shri Ram said, "Bhay binu hoye na preet"

Without fear, love and respect do not exist. But we must not live only in fear. We must not fear death, but understand it.

No matter how hard we try, death will come. So why die every single day out of fear?

Human beings are naturally drawn to beauty, even if there is something wrong hidden behind it. Life may run unjustly yet appear beautiful from outside. But death, the greatest truth of existence, never gets the dignity of being called beautiful.

Life has three major events- Birth, life, and death. Birth brings joy, life brings struggle, and death brings fear.

I remember an incident in a hospital. The moment the doctor gave the news, Sandeep ran out with excitement. He was so thrilled that instead of waiting for the lift, he sprinted down the stairs. At the gate, he almost collided with a stranger. From there, he rushed straight to a sweet shop, bought boxes of kaju katli, and returned to the hospital. He fed sweets to the guard at the gate first. Nearby, the same man whom he had almost bumped into earlier, he was standing quietly. Sandeep offered him sweets too. The man refused, but Sandeep insisted, "Come on! I've become a father after 12 long years! It's a moment of joy - please don't refuse."

The man accepted the sweet. Sandeep placed his hand on his shoulder and said, "Everything will be okay, brother." The man walked inside the hospital silently. His behavior seemed strange to Sandeep, so he asked the guard, "Is someone from his family very serious?". The guard said, "Not serious... his father passed away a little while ago. He's waiting for relatives to arrive."

Sandeep froze. His happiness dissolved instantly. Quietly, he walked back to the ward where his wife and newborn were waiting. In his mind, he kept repeating, "One man becomes a father after 12 years, another loses his father on the same day."

Aren't hospitals the strangest of places? Someone is overflowing with joy while someone else is drowning in grief.

Life is the same - everything happening here at the same time. Where you stand determines what life feels like celebration or sorrow. This is the rule of existence: life keeps moving. Someone arrives, someone leaves, but nothing stops.

If we fear death, we cannot truly live. Fear will not make life easier; it will only make it heavier. **The truth is that life has meaning because death exists.**

We make life difficult by fearing death, when instead we should wish for a healthy body and a meaningful life. And for meaning, we must keep trying with sincerity. When we try with true devotion, God and nature support us. The fear of death exists only because we do not understand it. The day we understand death is the say we will stop fearing it and actually start living. It is written in the Bhagavad Gita that "Death is the only undeniable truth of human life." And yet, even knowing this, man fears it and that fear destroys his present joys. The Gita is meant to be lived, not kept for one's final moments.

Someone said beautifully:

My body is made of soil;
my breaths are borrowed.
What ego should I have?
We are all just tenants in this world.

Even when God took birth as a human, He too had to leave one day. If the divine Himself follows the ultimate law of this world, then who are we to think otherwise? The Gita says that one must understand the cycle of birth and death, because the only absolute truth is death. Anyone who is born must leave eventually. The Gita teaches us to focus on our actions, not the results. "Karmaanubandheeni Manushyalokey"

Action is in our hands, not the outcome. So, when death is the ultimate truth, why search for evil? Why hold hatred toward anyone when all of us are destined for same end? **Perhaps if we understand death, we will rise above ego and illusions.** We will let go of jealousy, negativity, and destructive emotions. Believe me understanding death is the first step toward rising in life.

In simple words, death means ending. If there were no end, life would become a burden. The desire to live exists because life is finite. Imagine if death did not exist, mankind would be immortal. And immortality, in the wrong hands, could destroy the world. In the truest sense, it is death that teaches us renunciation, humanity and humility. So, accept the truth of death and move ahead in life. But how to move ahead? That is what the next twenty chapters entail.

2

The Beginning

Step into your potential,
and time will teach your critics
how to applaud.

My grandmother's house is the true name of my beginning. That courtyard where I learned to walk, where I learned to fall. I can never forget that courtyard. I can never forget those stories that taught me how to live. Everything I am today... is the gift of that beginning.

Once, I asked the CEO of a big company what she does when she faces a crisis. She smiled and said, "I simply go back to my childhood." I didn't understand. So, I asked, "What do you mean?" She said, "I just remember the basics — the things I learned as a child. Solutions to big problems are often very simple. But we disconnect ourselves from our roots and end up making small troubles appear huge."

It is important to remember your roots.

I still remember meeting the great actor, Pankaj Tripathi Ji at an event in Delhi. I reminded him of something he once said: "Who knew that once we learn to swim, we will drift away from the river?" At the same event, the Water Resources Minister of Bihar was also present. Pankaj ji said, "Yes, life is unpredictabl. Anything can change at any time. But since we are talking about rivers, I have just reminded the Honourable Minister that the very river in which we learned to swim, its flow has weakened. It needs attention."

He said it lightly and moved on to another topic but those words stayed with me. Think about it:

A man who now lives in Mumbai, hugely successful, known around the world, and busy with films, still cares about the river of his village - the river he left behind once he learned to swim. Pankaj Tripathi ji teaches the greatest lesson of life:

Never forget the soil of your village.

No matter where the world takes you never forget your nest.

I have seen people who hesitate to even mention the name of their village. I have seen people who now consider going back to their village as an insult. They think, "That was my past. I've left that behind." But I believe that whenever pride begins to overpower us, we should go back to those old lanes, those familiar crossroads, and to that tea stall where we once sat, dreaming of a better life.

Keep returning to your roots. Stay humble.

I will always remember Ayushmann Khurrana's words: Even a bird flying high in the sky knows there is no place to sit up there.

Always Remember Your Beginning

This is from when I started learning how to drive a car. The day I felt I could drive well, I asked my instructor, "Now I'm perfect, right?" He smiled and said,"No one is ever perfect. Every day on the road brings a new challenge." I couldn't understand. So, I asked him to explain. He said, "On Indian roads, no one knows who will appear from where or when. But remember one thing, never forget what you learned on the first day." Seeing the confusion on my face, he continued, "Just remember the basics:

"Keep your eyes steady, foot aware on the brake, speed under control, and your attention fully on the road."

If you remember your beginning, problems will never arrest you.

Today, after driving nearly one lakh kilometers, his words still guide me. Many people achieve success but fail to hold it for long. The biggest reason for their downfall is forgetting their beginning. The one who remembers where they started from protects their success throughout life.

Beginning From My Own Story

If I explain my own journey, I come from a middle-class family, but I was blessed with the values that every child must have: respect for elders, devotion, discipline and everything that helps a person grow from good to great.

I remember — I was always a dreamer. While studying in my hometown Bhawani Mandi, my father inspired me to study in Jawahar Navodaya Vidyalaya, Pachpahaar. There was an entrance exam for admission. I didn't get selected in 6th grade. In 8th, seats opened again — and with it, my dream came back. This time I cleared the exam. I was happy. But I was afraid too because I had always lived at home... How would I stay away?

I still remember when my father left me at the school hostel, my eyes filled with tears. I cried for a long time before reminding myself: "This is the beginning of those big dreams you've always seen." Navodaya Vidyalaya taught me what real life is. I was the child who scored 93% in 8th grade in Hindi medium. But now everything was in English. Suddenly, the student who always topped the class was now topping the list from the bottom. Homesickness grew.

And then, I met Bajrang Bhaiya. He was like a blessing in disguise. His room was filled with motivational quotes. He was the first motivational guide of my life.

He told me about his struggles, his family, and his hardships. After hearing his story, I realized my problems were very small. He taught me little techniques that helped me slowly transition from Hindi medium to English medium. I worked hard. In 9th, I scored 63% and in 10th, I reached 80%. And that is where I understood that there is only one shortcut to success and that is hard work.

> Someone said it beautifully:
>
> The beginning made for achieving the goal is itself half the achievement.

Truly, Beginning Is Powerful

First of all, set your goal. Start preparing for it. Stay consistent. And when you achieve it, never forget your beginning. Because your beginning keeps you grounded and prevents you from falling.

It is very important that your beginning is colossal. Let me share a story with you. Two friends came from different villages to a city to prepare for government exams. Both cleared and became collectors in different districts. Later, both grew disillusioned with government jobs and shifted to the corporate world. One started his own company while the other kept switching jobs. Over time, the one who built his company became very successful. The other kept searching for stability. One day, while job hunting, he came across his friend's company advertisement and decided to join him. Since they were old friends, he was offered a good salary and a high post.

One evening, while returning from a celebration, the friend who was now the employee asked his owner-friend, "We started the same way. Same villages, same preparation, and same career shift. Then, why are you the owner and I am the employee?"

The company owner replied, "Do you remember the day we were walking to the coaching centre and halfway I said we left the fan on in our room? I wanted to go back and switch it off. You said, 'Let it be. It's the landlord's headache.' You went ahead but I returned, switched off the fan, and then came." He paused.

"Even then, my thinking was of an owner. And yours was of a renter. When you treat everything as your own then Life rewards you. When the beginning is right then the results are right. **A tree grows tall only if its roots are strong."**

Why Beginning Matters?

Every great success story has one thing in common: the beginning. Sachin Tendulkar became a legend, but only because a little boy once dreamed of lifting the World Cup after watching the victory of '83. Without that beginning, there wouldn't be the 2011 World Cup. To reach your destination, you must take the first small step.

What Remains Is Only the Regret of Not Beginning

So many people say, "If only I had started then, I would be somewhere else today." Beginning may not guarantee success, but it guarantees growth, experience, transformation. The path to achievement always passes through beginning.

Why Do People Find it Difficult to Begin?

It is not that they don't know what to do. They know it well. But these things stop them:

1. No clear goal
2. Lack of confidence

3. Negative thinking
4. Always noticing flaws
5. And the biggest reason — laziness

If any of these are stopping you, then these 5 steps can change everything:

1. Identify clearly what you want
2. Change how you see success
3. Turn your values into your foundation
4. Step out of your comfort zone
5. Surround yourself with people who inspire you

3

Eklavya

#Someone said something profound

Sometimes being alone, and crying alone,
is what makes a person truly strong.

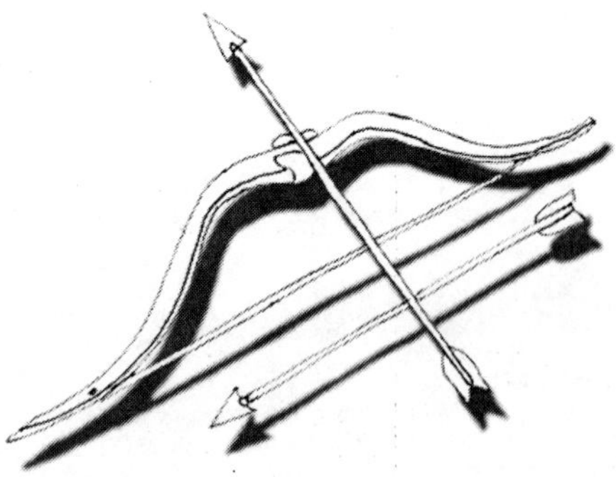

Eklavya, son of Hiranydhanu, had a burning desire to master archery from childhood. His eyes carried only one dream- to become the greatest archer under the guidance of Guru Dronacharya. Eklavya knew that Dronacharya taught only the princes, yet his heart held the firm belief that with true effort, even the impossible could be achieved.

When Eklavya gathered the courage to approach Dronacharya in the forests near the banks of the Ganga and asked to be accepted as a student, Dronacharya refused. He knew that teaching Eklavya could become a threat to his favourite student, Arjun. Eklavya was rejected but he did not lose heart.

He made a statue of Guru Dronacharya and accepted it as his teacher. From sunrise to sunset, every single day, he practiced archery in the silence of the forest. Every twig and every leaf became a part of his training. His dedication and discipline were extraordinary.

The stillness of the forest and the presence of nature became witnesses to his practice. His aim, his precision, and his skills sharpened, day by day. Eklavya not only educated himself, he transcended his own limitations.

Some months later, the Pandava and Kaurava princes accompanied Dronacharya on a hunting expedition. During their journey, their dog wandered into Eklavya's hermitage and began barking continuously, disturbing his practice.

Displaying his incredible skill, Eklavya shot several arrows in a way that sealed the dog's mouth without hurting him even a little. When the dog returned to Dronacharya and the princes, with its mouth closed by arrows, everyone was stunned by the craftsmanship. Dronacharya immediately understood that this was the work of a supremely skilled archer.

Dronacharya, in search of the archer, reached Eklavya. Seeing his guru arrive, Eklavya welcomed him with joy. But as Dronacharya learned of Eklavya's dedication and progress, a deep worry took root in him: If Eklavya continued like this, he would surpass Arjun. Dronacharya decided to ask for his guru dakshina and what he asked for left everyone shocked. He demanded Eklavya's thumb.

Without a moment's hesitation, Eklavya cut off his thumb and offered it to his guru. His sacrifice was not just an example of devotion. It was the ultimate expression of unshakable faith and surrender.

Even after losing his thumb, Eklavya did not abandon archery. He continued practicing and eventually mastered archery without it. In time, he became the king of the Nishad tribe and took his father's legacy forward. He built a powerful army, expanded his kingdom, and his courage and skill became widely known.

Eklavya's story is not just a tale of a warrior; it is an eternal symbol of sacrifice, dedication, and relentless effort.

It reminds us that true devotion never goes unrewarded. No matter how difficult the circumstances, if the heart is determined, success will surely come. His sacrifice, his discipline, and his courage will remain immortal - forever.

The Mahabharata never speaks of him again. But this character affected me deeply. Even while reading the ending of the Mahabharata, my mind kept returning to him. Strange, isn't it? How few people name their children after Eklavya. Most people forget the first chapter of the Mahabharata, but I feel the true essence of life was hidden right there. Everyone remembered Arjun, but they forgot the other disciple of Dronacharya the one who never entered the guru's ashram, yet learned everything by surrendering completely to his guru in spirit.

> Someone once said a beautiful thing:
>
> Sometimes being alone, and crying alone, is what makes a person truly strong.

Eklavya Taught Me the Art of Learning

From Eklavya, I learned that a teacher won't always appear in your life. You have to learn many things by yourself. When I went to boarding school, I had to do every little thing on my own. Growing up in a joint family, I never had the habit of doing things myself. When small tasks which were huge to me, came my way, I began to panic. That's when a senior came to me and said, "Brother, you've grown up now. No one will come and tell you that you've grown up. You'll have to learn many things yourself. Fall down, get up, and learn again."

When I dreamed of becoming a radio jockey in college, that journey, for me, was just like Eklavya's. Like him, I had gurus but they were far beyond my reach. Whether it was learning by listening or understanding the smallest details, I did it all on my own. Whenever I got rejected in auditions, I turned the feedback into my strength. Someone would say, "Improve your English," someone else would say, "Make your voice stronger." I listened to everything and learned. People from small towns will understand this very well: in big cities, nobody teaches you even how to step onto a mall escalator for the first time. You have to become your own Eklavya and learn it yourself. I learned the lifestyle of a big city exactly like Eklavya.

The Eklavya Inside Me Always Pushed Me Forward

When I got my first internship, I didn't even know how to talk in an office environment — nobody had ever taught me that. Once again, my inner Eklavya said, "We'll learn this too." When I played my self-recorded links for the RJ I admired, he said, "You've learned to speak like us! How?" I replied, "Just by listening." Whenever I would explain the tiny details of his own show to him, he would be shocked and ask, "Who taught you this?" I always said: "It's not just your show, I listened to every show that aired at your time. And that's how I learned what can make your show even better."

The Problem with Being an Eklavya

When people at the office began listening to me and asking for my suggestions, I felt I had achieved something. But being an Eklavya has one big problem: You never know where you've gone wrong. There's no one to point out your mistakes. You feel you're learning correctly; you feel you can't possibly be wrong, but you don't realize when you've taken a wrong turn. On my journey of being an Eklavya, I'm deeply grateful to all those mentors who guided me and showed me my shortcomings.

For a long time during my internship, I felt proud that I had learned so much just by listening to the radio. But soon I realized that being an Eklavya wasn't enough. I had to work on my weaknesses too.

1 September 2010 – A Day I Will Never Forget

This was the day I did my first radio show. At the beginning, I forgot everything, including the Eklavya inside me who had brought me this far. I started enjoying just being an RJ. I forgot that even after becoming an RJ, I had to remain an Eklavya because whatever I had learned was still so little. There was so much more to do, so much more to learn.When our State Head came for a station visit in Kota, he saw me chirpy and carefree. He understood instantly: "This boy thinks he's achieved enough but he doesn't realize the sky is still far away."

The next morning, after my show, he called me in. He asked the entire office to sit together, and he played my entire show in front of everyone. For the first time ever, my show was being heard collectively.People had always praised me individually, but that day I realized the difference between "good" and "truly great."

As my show played, the boss asked everyone to point out my flaws. One after another, people began listing my shortcomings.I kept writing them down.But when the first page of my diary filled up entirely with my mistakes, my tears fell on the page.That day I understood: Reaching the top and staying at the top are two very different things.

The Eklavya inside me silently thanked my boss that day, "Had you not shown me my flaws this way, I would have never realized how much I needed to grow."

What It Truly Means to Be an Eklavya

You've often heard that every successful person gets the same 24 hours, the same earth, the same sky, yet they do something that makes their name unforgettable.The simple reason: They awakened the Eklavya within themselves.They allowed their inner Eklavya to rise, to learn what no one taught them. Pick any great personality, read about their life, and you will find one common thing: each one of them focused on self-learning. Even when life lacked resources, even when they faced limitations, they dreamed big and worked endlessly to fulfil those dreams.They threw that stone with all their strength, even though no one had ever taught them how to throw it.

Self-learning is as essential as going to school or college.Many things in life are never taught; we learn them on our own. When a child grows up, many things are not taught to him; he simply observes and learns. The problem begins when we grow older: we forget the Eklavya within us. Being an Eklavya means dreaming even those dreams that feel out of reach, and building the passion needed to achieve them.

Messi Also Awakened the Eklavya Within

Born into a middle-class family, Lionel Messi is today considered one of the greatest footballers in the world.But his journey from the ground to the skies was far from easy.He began playing at a very young age. His grandmother was his biggest inspiration. His father gave him a football, and the little boy played with it day and night.The family's financial condition was weak, so Messi practiced constantly without any coach. At a very young age, Messi awakened the Eklavya within him.

At the age of 10, his grandmother passed away.At 11, he was diagnosed with growth hormone deficiency. He needed expensive medical treatment. Despite being extraordinarily talented, his local club refused to support his treatment. But neither Messi nor his parents gave up. Ignoring his illness, he kept playing and kept moving forward.

Through a talent hunt, FC Barcelona discovered him. They not only offered him a chance to join the club but they also agreed to cover all his medical expenses.And from that moment on, Messi never looked back. Today, he is one of the highest-earning footballers in the world. Messi had many reasons to stop but he awakened the Eklavya within him, and chose the path of success.

The Powerful Life Lessons Eklavya Teaches Us

I have learned from countless successful people that learning at every moment in life is essential. We never know how a small skill we learned today may help us tomorrow. And it's not necessary that we always need a teacher to teach us everything. With enough practice, we can master things on our own as well. Eklavya, who became greater than Arjun without anyone's guidance, taught us the true value of self-learning. Here are the five lessons I learned from Eklavya:

1. The True Meaning of Learning

In today's online world, learning seems easy. People watch videos and feel they've learned a lot even from people they've never met. But is that enough? No. Merely reading or watching something is not real learning. Real learning happens only when you apply that knowledge in your life.

2. **Compete With Yourself, Not Others**

Do you know the difference between Karna and Eklavya? Karna wanted to prove he was greater than Arjun. His competition was with someone else. But Eklavya's competition was with only one person: the version of himself from yesterday. We waste so much energy trying to defeat others when that same energy could make us better, if we focused on ourselves.

3. **Stay Away from Despair**

When Dronacharya rejected Eklavya, he didn't lose hope. He created his guru's statue and began practicing on his own. Life often throws failures and disappointments at us. Instead of losing heart, we must learn from Eklavya. Just find a new path and keep moving towards the goal.

4. **Self-Learning**

Not every phase of life gives us a Dronacharya. Sometimes, life demands that we learn on our own. That Art Of Learning without guidance is Self-Learning. Just as Eklavya practiced until he surpassed even Arjun, we too can achieve our goals with consistent efforts.

5. **Consistency**

To achieve excellence, consistency is crucial. Many people begin their journey with great excitement but they don't stay consistent. Eklavya teaches us that to master any field, consistency is non-negotiable. If we practice repeatedly and stay committed, success is

4

Perspective

#Someone said something profound

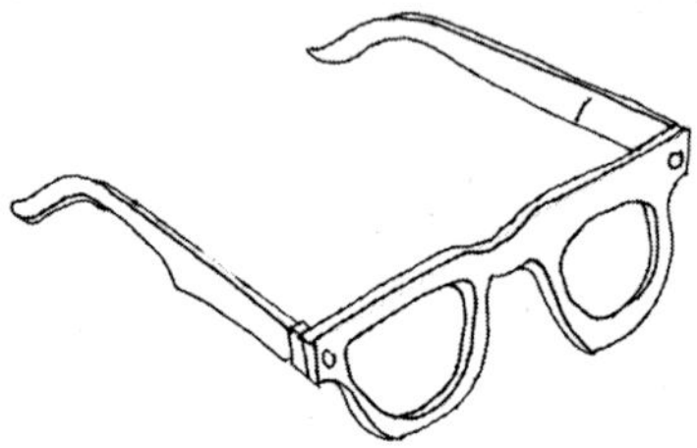

If you notice flaws in someone, talk to them;
but if you see flaws in everyone,
then talk to yourself.

You must have heard this saying: "What you think, you become." I don't know how much importance you personally give to this idea, but I have seen many successful people living by it. I know many such individuals who changed their perspective which eventually transformed their destiny. Remember, even the biggest transformations begin with the smallest efforts. And those efforts begin with your perspective; with your vision..

In our school, we had a teacher whom every student adored. His way of teaching was beautiful. One day, he asked me, "Tell me, which animal runs the fastest?" I replied, "Cheetah." Then he asked, "Which animal is the tallest?" I said, "The giraffe, with the long neck." He then asked, "And which animal is the largest in size?" I answered, "The elephant." But his next question carried the real lesson. He asked, "Then tell me, who is the king of the jungle?" All the children answered together, "The lion!" The teacher smiled and said, "The lion is not the fastest. It is not the tallest. It is not even the largest. And yet, the lion rules the jungle. Why?" He continued, "There is only one reason: the lion's perspective. The lion sees himself as the king. His vision and his attitude is what makes him the ruler of the jungle."

Our Vision Shapes Our World

We learn so much in our childhood, yet as we grow up, we slowly begin to forget it. In today's corporate language, you could say "we need reminders." And those reminders often come to us through the people who genuinely want to see us grow.

I have been in the media world for almost fourteen years now. I once had a boss whose perspective was different from everyone else. One day, he gave me a lesson that changed the way I think. In the beginning, I used to enjoy knowing what was happening in the office. Who left the company, who was planning to switch jobs etc. I loved these discussions.

One-third of my day would pass just talking about people. I believed office gossip was simply a part of life. I even liked knowing who arrived late, who left early. Then a new boss, Aditya Aman, joined the office. One day he asked me, "How long will you keep thinking like this?" I said, "Meaning?" He replied, "Every day you tell me he came late, she left early, he worked less. Do you think any of this benefits you?" I said, "No." He said, "If someone leaves early, that's management's concern. If someone comes late, that's also management's concern. You focus only on yourself. Leave management's job to management. First learn to manage yourself." Then he asked me one question that changed my life: "In an eight-hour job, do you work with full sincerity for all eight hours?" I said, "No." He said, "That's where you are losing. Manage yourself first. If you try to manage the whole world, you'll lose yourself." From that day, my perspective changed. I moved away from gossip and started focusing on myself. Now, if someone came late or left early, my heart would simply say, "They must have had a reason."

We don't spend time improving our perspective. Instead, we use the same limited perspective to damage our own lives. In reality, before we start any work, our mind has already finished half of it. If our vision is positive, our work naturally becomes sincere.

Your World Depends on Your Perspective

Your perspective decides whether your life will be filled with joy or sorrow. Everyone sees the same world differently. Some see a glass of water as half empty, while others see it as half full. Our thoughts depend entirely on our perspective. From my experience, a better perspective creates a better world.

Capability Alone Is Not Enough, Perspective Matters Too

To achieve success, ability is necessary, but so is the right attitude. You may be skilled, but if your perspective is negative, success will stay out of reach. Imagine you are a team leader. If you view your team with negativity, they will never be able to perform well because your thoughts influence them. Only a positive and encouraging attitude can take you to success.

Thoughts Depend Upon Perspective

Swami Vivekananda said: "It is our own mental attitude that makes the world what it is for us." Our thoughts have the power to make something beautiful or terrible. The whole world exists in our mind.

We must learn to see things in the right light. Often, we see someone and immediately decide whether they are good or bad. But if our perspective is narrow, we miss their goodness. Only with a positive mind can we recognize the good in others.

Perspective Can Change the World

Winston Churchill said that if you believe the world is full of negativity, you will only see negativity. But if you shift your perspective even a little, not only will the world but every person and every situation in your life begin to make sense, and you will find peace.

Perspective Shapes Character

Albert Einstein said: "Weakness of attitude becomes weakness of character." The way you think influences who you become. If you always look for mistakes in others, negativity slowly shapes your personality. A positive outlook, however, shapes a positive character.

The World Becomes Good When Our Perspective Is Good

As Earl Nightingale said, "The attitude we have toward others determines their attitude toward us." If you assume others are foolish, they form a similar image of you. If you assume you are among capable and good people, you will be respected.

The Difference Perspective Makes

People with positive thinking are eager to learn throughout life. They enjoy trying new things and are not afraid of mistakes. But those who think negatively avoid challenges because they fear discomfort. Such people resist change and stay stuck in the same mindset.

The Impact of Perspective

Your perspective affects your health, your relationships, your earning capacity, your ability to face challenges, in fact your entire life. With the right attitude, every problem becomes manageable. But if your thinking is wrong, even small issues look huge. Every home has at least one person who keeps the whole family hopeful. If you have a positive mindset, stress reduces and courage increases. Positivity helps you stay strong mentally and physically.

Perspective Makes Everything Easy

A king once built a grand palace. On the main gate, he placed a mathematical riddle. He announced that whoever solves the riddle and opens the gate would become his heir. Great mathematicians came but returned disappointed. On the final day, three people came. Two were renowned scholars carrying books. The third appeared like a simple seeker, carrying nothing. The scholars tried hard but failed. Then the seeker walked to the gate calmly, smiled, and simply pushed it. The gate opened. The king asked, "How did you solve it?" The seeker replied, "Before solving the riddle, I checked whether the riddle even existed."

Many times, in life, the problem is not real. We create it in our mind. Most of our problems exist only in our mind.

Intelligence Alone Is Not Enough

Stanford research by psychologist Carol Dweck proved that success depends more on mindset than IQ. People with a fixed mindset believe they cannot change, so challenges overwhelm them. But people with a growth mindset believe they can improve with effort, so they perform better even if their IQ is lower. Failure is simply a message: "This method didn't work. Try another."

5 Simple Ways to Improve Perspective

1. **Start Your Day Right**

   Begin your day with something that brings peace and clarity. It can be yoga, a good book, music, or a calm breakfast. A peaceful morning sets a powerful tone.

2. **Speak Positively**

   Use positive words about yourself and others. Your language shapes your thoughts, and your thoughts shape your life.

3. **Avoid Gossip**

   Gossip creates stress and negativity. Distance yourself from it. It protects your mind and increases your focus.

4. **Express Appreciation**

   Take a moment daily to feel grateful for the people and blessings in your life. Gratitude strengthens positivity.

5. **Practice Meditation**

   Meditation helps you stay centered and calm. When your mind is steady, challenges feel lighter.

5

Hope

#Someone said something profound

As long as the branches remain,
leaves will return and flowers will bloom.
If these days are hard,
better days will come too.

It was one of those evenings when I was waiting for my father with a heart full of hope. Papa will bring me a new bat today. Every child knows that excitement. Mobile phones hadn't taken over our world yet, so little joys, like a new bat, could easily make our day. Today, perhaps that thrill for outdoor games isn't the same anymore. I was really upset that evening when Papa didn't keep his promise. He had never broken a promise before, and that day too, he had clearly said he would bring a new bat. But it didn't happen. Papa came home very late, and when he finally arrived, his hands were empty. I didn't speak to him that evening. I stubbornly decided that I'll only eat once the bat arrives, and I'll only talk to Papa after that.

That's when my mother explained softly, "Today, senior officers visited Papa's office. He couldn't even have lunch." Listening to her, I went to Papa with tears in my eyes, said sorry, and convinced him to have dinner. Papa smiled and said, "What's there to cry about?" I replied, "Because you broke my hope, Papa. That's why I'm sad." He placed his hand on my head and said, "Just wait for tomorrow evening." The next day, Papa came home early and in his hands was a beautiful, stunning bat. Something far better than I had imagined. I thought he'd bring a normal bat, but this one was twice as good as my expectations.

Life works the same way. Sometimes our hopes shatter, and sometimes life gives us double than what we hoped for. They say the world runs on hope. "Tomorrow morning I'll finish the project at office" that's hope. Those who are in love think, "Tomorrow I'll see that beautiful face again. Tomorrow I will confess my feelings" that too is hope."

Hope is the strength that keeps our life meaningful and moving. The whole world, every thought, every action we take, everything rests on some hope. Hope is the spark that lights up the darkness.

Whenever we begin something, there is always a silent belief inside us that the outcome will be good. That belief is hope. Even breathing is based on hope that the next moment will bring something new. Even the alarm we set for the next morning is hope. If life had no hope, everything would freeze. Humans would have no reason to live. Hope is the fuel that pushes us forward, even through the toughest times.

"Hope" may be a small word, but it holds immense power. With hope, the biggest problems find solutions. They say even if you lose everything, but you haven't lost hope, then you haven't lost anything at all. That's why no matter what situations we face in life, we must always hold on to the hope of better days. My mother always told me, "Beta, another name for life is struggle. So never lose the hope of living every moment, moving forward, and becoming better." And following her words, even today, I wake up every morning with the hope of being better than yesterday.

Situations won't always favor us. Many times, challenges appear that we never even imagined. Standing strong in such times isn't easy but that is when hope becomes our greatest support. **When courage begins to fade, we don't need blind faith; we just need to strengthen our hope.**

Famous poet, Bashir Badr beautifully said:

No effort ever truly goes in vain,
Even if you don't reach the destination,
Your distance from it surely decreases.[1]

---

1 कोई भी कोशिश नाकाम यूँ जाती नहीं
मंज़िलें ना भी मिलीं तो फ़ासले घट जाएँगे

Keep Your Hopes Alive

Hope shouldn't only be placed in others, it must also be placed in oneself. When you hope for yourself, the chances of disappointment decrease because you work with your whole heart to fulfil that hope. And even if that hope breaks sometimes, confidence helps us find a new hope, a new path, and we begin again.

In the 1950s, Professor Curt Richter conducted a famous psychological experiment on drowning rats - a study that can give new strength to the hopeless and defeated. His experiment proved that even in the toughest circumstances, one must never give up hope.

Richter put rats in a bucket of water to see how long they would swim before giving up. Some rats swam for 10 minutes, some for 20, and then drowned. Later, he changed the experiment. He placed a rat in water, and just before it drowned, he rescued it. After a while, he put the same rat back in the water.

This time, something astonishing happened. Richter expected the rat to give up within minutes But instead, that rat swam for 72 hours straight. Why? Because now the rat had hope that someone would save it again. This was called the Hope Experiment.

And that's how life is - challenges will keep coming but every challenge teaches us something new. We just need to spread our arms wide and face them.

Once a person asked Swami Vivekananda, "What is worse than losing everything?" He replied, "Losing the hope that can help you regain everything." This message holds deep truth; no matter what you lose, never lose hope.

Someone rightly said, **"between your past and your tomorrow, only hope stands and encourages you to move forward."**

Hope Means — All is Well

Hope is that force which brings a ray of light even in the darkest times. It tells us that no matter how dark today seems, tomorrow the sun will rise with new light. That's what "All is well" truly means.

When we say all is well, it does not mean there are no problems. It means we are ready to face them, and we believe that in the end, everything will be okay. This mindset frees us from fear and worry. It helps us look at life with a positive lens. But with hope, patience and effort are equally important. Just saying all is well isn't enough. We must keep working. When hope walks hand-in-hand with effort, the impossible becomes possible.

That's why, at every turn in life no matter how hard the circumstances get, we must never let go of hope. When we say that hope means all is well, we are basically filling ourselves and others with positivity and confidence. It gives us strength to rise every time we fall. Hope reminds us that every ending is just a new beginning. Keep hope alive in your heart and live life with the spirit of "All is well."

Someone said it beautifully:

If branches remain, flowers and leaves will return.
If today is bad, tomorrow will be better.

A man once got lost in a desert. His condition was terrible. His food was finished. He hadn't had a drop of water in two days. He knew his end was near. Yet, somewhere inside, a small hope told him that God would save him and thus, he kept walking.

After walking endlessly, he saw a hut in the distance. He wondered, "Is this real or just another illusion?" But it was his last hope. Gathering all his strength, he walked towards it. When he reached, the hut was real but completely deserted. He stepped inside. There, he found a hand pump. He quickly worked on the pump, but it was dry. Exhausted, he fell to the ground. Then he noticed a bottle hanging from the roof. He grabbed it. It was filled with water. Just when he was about to drink it, he saw a note attached to it, "Use this water to prime the pump. And please refill the bottle before leaving."

Now he was torn. If he poured the water into the pump and it didn't work, he would die. But if it worked, he would have endless water. After much thought, he poured the water into the pump. Then he began pumping once, twice, thrice and suddenly cold, sweet water gushed out. His joy was immeasurable. He drank to his fill, refilled the bottle, and hung it back. Just as he was leaving, a thought struck him. He ran back, grabbed the paper, and added another line: "Trust me - this really works."

In childhood, whenever someone was going through a tough time, I heard people say, "Everything will be fine." Whether things actually turned out fine or not, I don't know. but those four words gave comfort. They gave strength. Even today, those same four words push the world forward. In truth, they are the biggest words of hope. The world is full of people who still hold onto hope. Yet, we need more such bearers of hope who encourage others, who uplift others, and help keep their hopes alive. Hope is not just a feeling; it is the foundation of life. We must never let our hope break. It is the force that shows us light even in complete darkness.

Faiz Ahmad Faiz wrote a powerful line:

The heart is not without hope, merely unsuccessful.
The night of sorrow is long but only a night after all.[2]

Why Expectations from Others Hurt

Most of the pain and disappointment in our lives comes from the expectations we place on others. We overlook this truth but understanding it is essential for peace and contentment. Humans are social beings. We depend on our relationships. So, it's natural to expect things from others; small expectations like someone arriving on time, or big ones like expecting someone else to solve our problems. But when these expectations remain unfulfilled, they give birth to hurt.

We forget that every person has their own limitations and priorities. We expect them to behave as we think they should. When they don't, we feel our emotions aren't valued. But the truth is people's thoughts and circumstances may be completely different from what we imagine.

How to Reduce Expectations from Others

1. **Focus on Yourself:**

   Build your own life. Don't make others the source of your happiness.

2. **Practice Acceptance:**

   Everyone is different. Accept their choices and priorities.

---

2 दिल ना-उम्मीद तो नहीं नाकाम ही तो है
लम्बी है ग़म की शाम मगर शाम ही तो है

3. **Set Boundaries:**

   Healthy expectations prevent disappointment and teach you what is realistic.

4. **Meditate and Self-reflect:**

   It helps you gain control over your emotions and focus on inner peace.

5. **Practice Gratitude:**

When you notice the good in others, negative expectations naturally fade.

Expectations aren't wrong. Expecting from the wrong people is what hurts. Some people say, "Don't have expectations at all, that's the secret to happiness." But they don't understand humans don't survive on oxygen alone; hope is essential. Even if humans find life on another planet, they still can't live there without hope. In fact, the search for life on other planets is humanity's biggest hope from science.

6

Dilemma

#Someone said something profound

The world is neither as cruel as our fears,
nor as kind as our blind trust.

One day, I was watching an interview of one of the finest actors in Hindi cinema, Pankaj Tripathi Ji. He said, "The world is not as good as we assume it to be, and the world is not as bad as we sometimes believe it is. The world is a shade of grey."

Director Anurag Kashyap's movie Manmarziyaan had a song written by lyricist Shellee "Kaala na safed hai ishqe da rang yaara, grey wala shade hai..." Love is neither black nor white, it is a shade of grey..."

And in life, there are moments that go beyond right and wrong; such moments define what life actually is. That bitter reality—which neither matches what we have learned from books nor what the world has taught us so far. Life that keeps happening to us even when we don't want it to. Life that breaks the definitions of right and wrong and silently tests our mind. The world is busy judging us,and we are busy trying to paint the grey inside us into white.

There is a Chinese philosophical concept, Yin-Yang, which describes two opposite yet interconnected forces. Where there is white, there is also a small black dot. And where there is black, there is also a small white dot. It tells us that the world is not as bad as we think when we turn our back on it, and not as good as we think when we blindly trust everyone. There is good in this world, yes. But there is also a little evil. We meet all kinds of people in this world. We just have to decide whom we choose to give importance to.

There's a story my teacher once narrated in class that was beyond right and wrong. A story explaining the complexities of life. A story that shows some decisions cannot be judged by the world outside. Because some choices can only be understood by the one who made them.

So, story of the teacher goes like this

Once, a large ship met with a major accident while sailing in the middle of the ocean. The captain ordered everyone to evacuate. Among the passengers was a young couple. When their turn came to get onto the lifeboat, they saw that only one seat was left. At that moment, the man pushed the woman aside and jumped into the boat. Standing on the sinking ship, the woman shouted a single sentence to her husband as he drifted away. At this point, the teacher stopped and asked the class, "What do you think the wife yelled?" Most students immediately replied, "She must have screamed: 'I hate you! You selfish man!' because he left her alone to die." But one boy sat quietly. The teacher asked him, "What do you think?" The boy said softly, "I think she said... 'Take care of our child.'"

The teacher was surprised. "Have you heard this story before?" she asked. The boy replied, "No, ma'am. But that's what my mother said to my father before she passed away." The teacher paused... and then said gently, "Your answer is correct."

The story continued. The ship sank and the woman died. But the man survived and devoted the rest of his life in raising his daughter. Years later, after the man passed away, his daughter found his diary while cleaning. And there she discovered. At the time of that ship journey, her mother was suffering from a terminal illness. She had only a few days left to live. In such a moment of crisis, the father had to make a terrible decision. He wrote: "Without you, there is no meaning to my life. I wanted to drown in the ocean with you. But when I thought of our child...I had to leave you behind."

As the daughter read this, her tears would not stop. Because all her life she had blamed her father. All her life she believed he was the selfish one. All her life she never understood his pain.

The truth was always beyond what her eyes could see. Beyond right or wrong. Sometimes life is so complicated that only the person experiencing it truly understands it. It's like sitting in the stadium and judging a cricketer. Only the one facing the ball knows why he couldn't hit that last six.

If there is life, there will be dilemmas

A dilemma is a situation where you must choose between two paths. But choosing one means breaking another rule you yourself believed in.I felt this for the first time in school.A friend asked me to copy homework. I refused. But he still copied. And then the second dilemma arose, "Should I tell the teacher or not? If I tell, the friendship may break. If I don't, he may rely on shortcuts forever." Finally, I told his elder sister. She explained things lovingly. I hope he never chose the wrong path again. This may sound simple. But as you grow older, dilemmas grow bigger with you.

Dilemmas break a person from inside. In today's fast life, social pressure, family expectations, and fear of judgment: all trap the mind. How do we deal with it?

1. Yoga, Pranayama, and Meditation

2. Stay away from unnecessary arguments

3. Talk not only to yourself but also to the person involved

If there is a dilemma, there is a solution too.

According to Patanjali: "Vitarka badhane pratipaksha bhavanam." When conflicting thoughts arise, bring forth the opposite emotion. Where there is anger, bring compassion. Where there is hatred, bring love. Difficult? Yes. Impossible? No.

Sometimes negative thoughts dominate the mind. And then we start seeing problems in every opportunity. This inner conflict leads to confusion. Which direction should we choose? In such moments, contemplation becomes your medicine. **When anger arises - think of kindness. When someone speaks harshly - smile, because in that moment, your response is your victory. Life will always have dilemmas.** But how we respond defines who we become.

7

Struggle

#Someone said something profound

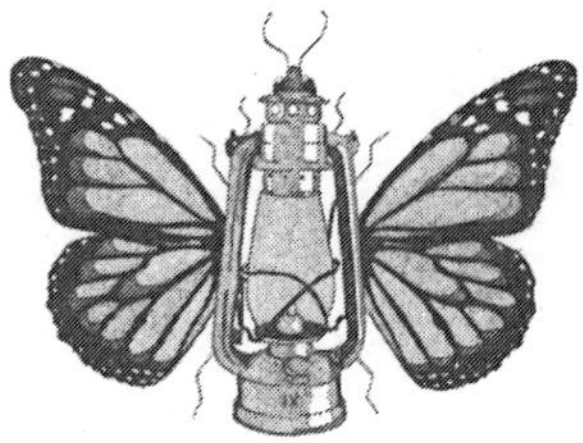

Keep trying.
The last key in the bunch
often opens the door.

In the early days of my radio career, I had to interview a very big celebrity. Deep inside, I was nervous. I had read about his life, prepared my questions, and was fully ready. So the moment the interview began, I asked my first question: "How much struggle did you go through in your life? How difficult were those days?" He replied, "I never struggled." I panicked even more; he was outright denying it. Somehow, I held myself together and said, "But you spent nights on railway stations in Mumbai... survived on pav... went from one film director to another, and often returned after hearing a 'no'. Isn't that struggle?" That famous personality gently placed his hand on my shoulder and said,"No, my friend. That wasn't struggle. That was the beginning of my journey. It was an essential part of it. If that phase hadn't come, I would've never been able to enjoy success."I asked, "How?" He said, "Because that phase showed me what I truly wanted. It showed me my purpose. When I used to visit different studios every day, give auditions, meet directors, and return home after hearing another 'no' every night, I asked myself, 'Do I really want to become an actor?' And every night the answer was the same. 'Yes. This is exactly what I want. I want to be an actor.' And when I finally became one, when I finally got work, my heart was happy and my soul felt fulfilled, because I had received what I had desired with complete sincerity."."

That day I learned the real definition of struggle. I realized that **struggle is just one stop on the journey; it is a part of it.If someone says, "I'm going through struggle," understand that a great story is being written.** Even when I rewind my own life, I remember those internship days when I used to walk to the office, when I had no certainty of lunch or dinner, when sometimes a packet of ₹5 biscuits became dinner. But even then, only one thought echoed in my mind: "I want to become a Radio Jockey." I never thought of it as a struggle. Because I knew this is supposed to happen. This is a part of my journey.

But success doesn't appear early in the journey. Problems come, struggle comes, and for some people, that phase never seems to end. There was a senior in my Jawahar Navodaya Vidyalaya boarding school. I always noticed he worked harder than everyone else. When I asked him, he told me about his home situation with tears in his eyes. A few days back, when I reconnected with him, I asked how he was doing. He said, "Just caryying on." but when I asked him again, he told me the whole story. After school, he went to Kota to prepare for medical entrance exams. His family spent all their savings, and he missed the cut-off by just a few marks. People taunted him. So he left studies, returned to the village, and started farming. For clearing old debts, the land had to be sold. After that he somehow moved to the city and started with a small job in a private company. He said, "Brother, my entire life is a struggle." That day, I wondered: 'What really is struggle? How do we define it?' Its meaning depends entirely on the person and the phase they are in.

There's a story of Gautam Buddha that teaches us how to handle such situations. Once, while Buddha was giving a sermon, a farmer came to him. "I have many problems," he said. "Someone told me you can solve them all." He started: "My first problem is my work. I like farming, but sometimes there's no rain and my crop dries up. Last year, we almost starved. Sometimes it rains too much, and I don't get the yield I want."

Buddha listened patiently. The farmer continued, "My next problem is my personal life. I have a good wife, but sometimes she bothers me so much that I feel like running away." Buddha stayed silent.

"My two kids also trouble me sometimes, and sometimes they're loving. The list of my problems is very long." After saying everything, he waited for Buddha's solution." But he was shocked when Buddha said, "I'm sorry, but I cannot help you."

He was furious. He had come a long way, wasted his time, and now Buddha had no answers? That's when Buddha said, "Look, everyone in this world has their own set of problems. In fact, all of us have ninety-nine problems that we cannot do anything about. You solve one, another will appear. You'll fix your son's health and your father will fall sick. Life is like this." The farmer exploded, "What kind of enlightened man are you? You have no solutions at all!" Buddha smiled and said,"I can solve your hundredth problem." The farmer asked,"What is that?"Buddha said,"You want a life without problems." And that I can fix not by removing your problems, but by helping you stop expecting a problem-free life. As long as there is breath, there will be problems. That's how nature works.

There are lines by the great poet Maithilisharan Gupt that I always remember:

> Those who bloom like flowers amidst thorns,
> their fragrance and glory spread everywhere.[1]

If life is there, there will be struggle. So, first of all, don't live life with fear, live it with courage and happiness. It's also true that struggle cannot have a fixed definition. Everyone's life is different; everyone's challenges are different. So, how can struggles be the same? In life, we face many ups and downs, and for me, fighting

---

1 जितने कष्ट कंटकों में हैं जिनका जीवन सुमन खिला
गौरव गंध उन्हें उतना ही यत्र तत्र सर्वत्र मिला

through them and moving forward is what "struggle" truly means. Behind the success of every successful person lies their struggle. Struggle makes a person strong, no matter how weak they may be.

You must have heard, "The greater the struggle, the greater the victory." But words and reality are worlds apart.When tough times arrive, we often lose courage. That's when we can draw inspiration from those who have struggled and seen the positive outcomes of it. Struggle builds character. It shapes who we become in the future. **A small plant, too, becomes a tree only after enduring every season.** And without struggle, no one would feel any excitement or joy in life. Just as you cannot understand sweetness without tasting bitterness, you cannot understand the meaning of life without struggle.

You must have heard the story of the cocoon and the butterfly. A man once wanted to help a struggling butterfly and cut open the cocoon. He did it out of kindness, not knowing that the butterfly's struggle inside the cocoon was what strengthened its wings. That tiny hole is God's way of preparing the butterfly to fly. When it emerges on its own, only then can it soar. We unnecessarily fear struggle, but I see it as training, just like learning to drive a car. You need training, tests, and a license so you can drive safely later. And it's true, people who get things without struggle never value anything. Give an expensive phone to a child and he will never understand the hard work his father put in to buy it.

Someone said a beautiful thing -

Life is the courage to dream again
after a dream breaks into pieces.

The Path to Success Passes Through Struggle

World-famous author J.K. Rowling faced many hardships but never stopped struggling and stayed honest with her work. She often says that she learned from her adversities, that failures are essential in life. Infosys co-founder Narayana Murthy faced several failures. His first business shut down within a year and a half. After working for five years in another company, he started Infosys and today, it stands tall. Arunima Sinha, who lost a leg in an accident, never gave up. She kept struggling, kept fighting and today, she holds the record for conquering the Himalayas. From her, we learn that **instead of grieving over what is missing, if we hold the hand of struggle, every dream becomes possible.**

Bigger Success Requires Bigger Struggle

The moment a desire is born, struggle begins. A small child makes so much effort to reach a toy on the table - tiptoeing, using a stick, trying again and again and when he finally gets it, his smile carries the essence of his struggle. As we grow older, our desires grow, and so do our struggles. We work hard, face difficulties, and slowly understand that life has no meaning without struggle. Sadly, instead of teaching the importance of struggle to the next generation, we try to shield them from it. That's why they dream big but lack the courage to achieve those dreams. It is our responsibility to share our stories of struggle to inspire them not just to dream, but to work for those dreams.

The Spiritual Meaning of Struggle

"Life itself means struggle" - a line my mother always loved. Once, I asked her to explain it. She said: "In a person's life, struggle is constant. Everyone is fighting their own battles. But the greatest struggle is the one within the struggle to stay disciplined, to keep away from your own weaknesses,t o control your mind and desires. That is the biggest struggle of all." That is the battle where you defeat your own flaws and walk on the path of goodness, where the purification of the soul begins. Keep struggling. Keep moving on the path of success. You have my heartfelt wishes.

8

Worry

#Someone said something profound

Don't take people's words too seriously; People ask if guavas are sweet before buying them and then eat them sprinkled with salt.

The end of Chinta (Worry) is Chintan (Contemplation). And I believe that wherever contemplation exists, true life exists. Perhaps, right now, while reading this book, you are worrying about how to make peace with the friend you fought with two days ago. Or maybe your worries concern family relationships, or money. But remember, merely worrying can never be the solution but thinking about the solution can actually take you there. We often get stuck in events, tangled so tightly, like a kite caught in a distant tree during Makar Sankranti.

If worry is poison, contemplation is nectar. If worry is death, contemplation is life. Learning from your past mistakes and planning a better future - both are possible only through contemplation. Look around you: those who suffer from chronic worry always appear unhappy, while those who practice contemplation appear peaceful. All the great personalities of the world strengthened themselves through contemplation. They made contemplation their companion, not worry. You too, from today - from this very moment - should make contemplation your companion. Very soon, you will see yourself transforming from good to exceptional in whatever you do.

Doership and Contemplation: A Spiritual Insight

Worry is born from the feeling of being the doer. As long as you believe that every event in your life is solely the result of your effort, the burden of worry will remain in your mind. But the moment you truly understand that you are not the real doer - that everything is unfolding through God's will and the laws of karma - then worry dissolves on its own.

Ego creates creates the illusion of doership. Ego says: I did this. I am doing this. I will do this." But when you look within and recognise the deeper truth, it becomes clear that every event in life is - in a way, pre-written - the result of your past actions and destiny.

Understanding the impermanence of the world is one of the greatest truths of life. Once you accept this, attachment, illusion, and false ego begin to fade away. You begin to realize that everything is momentary, and that one day we must leave everything behind.

True peace and contentment arise only when you let go of the ego of being the doer and accept every situation with grace. From this **acceptance emerges a deep love that connects you with every being and with nature itself.** This love is the ultimate truth. To experience it, one must release ego and selfishness.

So, in every situation of life, understand the divine play of God. Fill your heart with love. And make every day peaceful and joyful. This is the true art of living.

The King's Worry and the Sage's Contemplation

Long ago, there lived a powerful king who was always drowned in worry about his kingdom. "What if enemies attack? What if famine strikes—then how will my people survive? Am I even a good king?" These worries troubled him so much that he couldn't sleep at night.

To find relief, the king invited a renowned sage to his court. The sage arrived calm, wise, and serene. The king bowed and said,

"Gurudev, I am always worried about my kingdom, my people, and the future. Please show me the path to be free from this worry."

The sage smiled and said, "Maharaj, I will certainly give you a solution, but first, I have a small task for you."

The sage handed the king an empty bowl. "Fill this bowl with oil and walk around your palace with it. But remember, not a single drop should spill."

The king accepted the challenge. He filled the bowl and walked carefully, eyes fixed on the oil, too afraid to look away. Finally, he returned and proudly said, "Gurudev, look, I didn't spill a single drop."

The sage asked, "When you were walking with the bowl, did you notice the beauty of your palace gardens?" The king said, "No. My attention was entirely on the bowl."

The sage smiled. "Maharaj, this is the difference between worry and contemplation. When your mind is stuck only on the problem (like the oil), you cannot see the beauty of life, nor the solutions available. That is worry. But if you look at the problem with a calm mind and seek its solution, that becomes contemplation."

The sage continued, "**Perform your duties, but don't let them weigh so heavily on your mind that you lose the joy of living.** To solve problems, you need calmness and contemplation, not unnecessary worry."

The king understood his mistake. He thanked the sage and decided to abandon worry and embrace contemplation.

Worry destabilizes the mind and pulls you away from solutions, while contemplation steadies the mind and shows you the right path. Leaving worry and adopting contemplation is the true art of life.

Someone said something truly wonderful:

> Don't take people's words too seriously; People ask if guavas are sweet before buying them and then eat them sprinkled with salt.

Worry and Contemplation: Two Perspectives

Worry is like a pyre that keeps burning a person from within. Contemplation is like a soothing rainfall, calming the inner fire and bringing stability to the mind. Worry drags a person into darkness; contemplation shows the path towards light. Worry confuses a person and pushes them toward the wrong path, while contemplation guides them in the right direction.

Worry breaks a person mentally and physically. **Contemplation is a light that helps them learn from their mistakes and move forward.** Worry is tied to fear and uncertainty. Contemplation symbolizes foresight and confidence.

Simply put, worry burdens the mind; contemplation enlightens it. **Avoid worry and embrace contemplation, that is the true mantra for living the right way.**

Contemplation has no age. From children to elders, everyone contemplates. Their subjects may differ. An elderly person contemplates how to live the rest of life peacefully. A young person contemplates how to build a prosperous future. Contemplation is not only for the future. Sometimes, reflecting on the past and learning from it can make the present joyful. And contemplating your present actions lays a strong foundation for the future.

Often, we struggle to decide what is most important work, family, friends, or ourselves. We feel confused and troubled.

Contemplation helps us find answers to these questions. It gives purpose to life and helps us achieve our goals.

Mystery of Three Envelopes

For 10 years, Mudit had been working in the same company for 10 years. Despite his efforts and dedication, he felt stuck. He worried constantly about his growth. One day, at his wife's suggestion, he applied for new jobs. He soon got selected at a multinational company - not just selected, but appointed as the manager, the head of the team.

On his first day, he noticed that the old boss was retiring. After the farewell, the old boss called Mudit into his cabin.

He handed him three envelopes and said:

"Keep these envelopes safe. When you face your first big crisis, open the first envelope; it contains a solution. If the problem returns, open the second. And if it returns again, open the third."

Mudit kept them carefully. A few months later, conflicts arose within his team. Not knowing what to do, he remembered the envelopes.

He opened the first one. Inside it was written: "Blame everything on the previous boss." Mudit told his team, "These issues are the result of mistakes made by the previous management. Now we will focus on fixing them." The team calmed down.

Months later, another conflict arose. He opened the second envelope. Again, it read: "Blame everything on the boss before the previous boss." He did exactly that and, once again, the issue settled. After some time, a third crisis came. This time, he opened the last envelope. Inside it was written: “Your time is up. Prepare three new envelopes and give them to your successor.”

Mudit finally understood that he had been escaping responsibility by blaming others, never truly solving the problems. Leadership means contemplation, not worry. It means working on solutions, not wasting time in excuses.

“Worry only magnifies the problem, while contemplation gives solutions. Spend time working, not making excuses. No matter how big the problem is, solutions emerge only through contemplation and effort.”

How to End Worry?

Creativity is born from contemplation, and overthinking is born from worry. Overthinking is never beneficial. It weakens us over time. To overcome it, we must understand where it begins. Here are five points to understand the roots of overthinking and how to remove the same:

1. **Understand Your Trigger Point:**

   Every person has a mental point at which they start overthinking. Once you identify that, you'll find the solution. And if your environment is negative, change it, because in overthinking, no one can help you except yourself. Surround yourself with positive people and a positive environment.

2. **Don't Chase Perfection:**

   Perfection is good, but always running behind perfection is painful. Some people want everything perfect. When things don't go their way, they blame themselves or others and that's where overthinking begins. Focus on doing your best instead of chasing perfection. Keep your mind in the present; it makes your today powerful, and if today is good, then tomorrow will also be beautiful.

3. **Don't Isolate Yourself:**

   Many people think being alone helps them, or that they prefer solitude. But too much isolation leads to overthinking. Being away from friends and family can harm your relationships and mental health. If you feel alone, go meet someone, take a walk, or meditate, but don't leave yourself alone in your thoughts.

4. **Make Writing Your Friend:**

   If you can't express your thoughts to someone, write them down in a diary. Writing releases your thoughts from your mind and reduces overthinking. What you keep in your mind stays heavy; what you write down becomes lighter.

5. **Learn to Forgive:**

   Learn to forgive yourself and others. Overthinking often begins when you think excessively about others' actions. This leads to negativity. Forgiveness brings peace. It is an act of great virtue.

Where Contemplation Exists:

- In listening and understanding good thoughts
- In reading and applying what you read
- In devotion, whether at a temple or in your garden
- In regular yoga and meditation

Contemplation is not a medicine you take for a few days and get cured. It is a part of daily life. Just as the body needs exercise to stay healthy, the mind needs contemplation to stay healthy. Still water gets spoiled; similarly, a still mind becomes dull. **Contemplation activates the mind, keeps it thinking, keeps it alive.**

Sometimes life overwhelms us with challenges, and a deep darkness covers the mind. Contemplation becomes the inner lamp that helps us find light again. When difficulties surround you from all sides, contemplation is what gives you clarity. Sit with yourself for a while. Talk to yourself. Understand your problems and contemplate. Even if you don't find an immediate solution, you'll gain the strength to face your challenges. Contemplation leads you toward solutions. Worry leads you only toward more worry. Always remember: Worry creates overthinking. Contemplation creates creativity. The choice is yours.

9

Jealousy

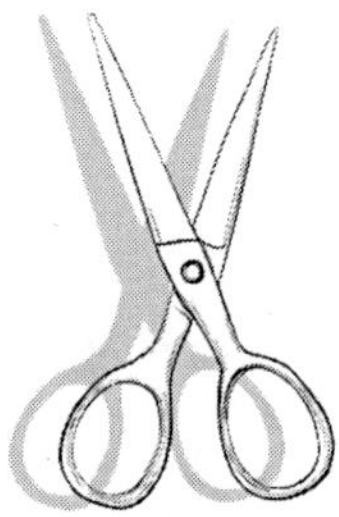

My Friend, be like a Lamp.
It doesn't burn for itself, it burns for others.

The largest volcano in the world stands in Hawaii, USA. Its name is Mauna Loa, rising 9,170 feet tall. It is an active shield volcano, and its lava flows in a smooth, fluid stream. But I have come to believe that there is a volcano far bigger, more dangerous, and more active than Mauna Loa - one that lives inside every human being. Its name is Jealousy. And when jealousy intensifies, it transforms into malice. Jealousy is that feeling of burning from within. It arrives even when we do not invite it. And as long as jealousy remains, peace can never find a place in the heart, because the world around us will continue to thrive, grow, and celebrate. And if we keep feeding jealousy, the fire will not burn others; it will burn us. If you keep your inner volcano active, there will only be lava — anger, unrest, and suffering. Every joy around you will feel like a personal loss. Instead, **if you start feeling happiness in the joy of others, something amazing will happen, and you will experience a rare kind of tranquility**

But before anything else, we must understand: What is jealousy?

Jealousy is a feeling born out of comparison. Whenever a person compares themselves to someone else, someone's qualities, lifestyle, wealth, personality, habits, and finds themselves lacking, a burning sensation arises inside. That burning is jealousy. So it's true: Jealousy happens only to those who cannot celebrate the success of others. Jealousy happens only to those who are behind, not to the ones who are ahead.

> Someone once said it beautifully:
>
> People talk behind your back only because they are already behind you.

Some sayings will always stand the test of time, even if we make a colony on the planet Mars. Like this one by Kabir:

> Wood turns to coal in fire,
> coal turns to ash again;
> I am burned by my sins so completely
> that neither coal nor ashes remain.[1]

This is jealousy. Such a feeling that comes in people's hearts is not from any marketplace. It is born silently within, like a slow-burning volcano.

The Four Sources of Jealousy

1. When someone grows more successful than you.
2. When failure or disappointment grips your life.
3. When others criticize or belittle you.
4. When you miss out on something important while others achieve it.

When a child is born, the mind is pure. But as we grow, layers of impurities gathers within us. And often, our parents themselves unknowingly plant the first seeds of jealousy. When a parent says: "The neighbor's child has better clothes because their father earns more," the child not only learns jealousy, but also learns to consider false stories as truth.

The Story of a Man and God

---

1 लकड़ी जल कोयला भई, कोयला जल भई राख,
मैं पापन ऐसी जली, कोयला भई ना राख

Once, a man prayed so sincerely that God appeared before him. The man said, "I want many things, but I want to ask for them daily. So please come every day." God agreed, but He too placed a condition: "Whatever you ask for, I will give you. But I will give double of it to your neighbors." The man agreed.

That day, he asked for a car. When he went outside, his new, shiny car was waiting for him. But his neighbors had two cars. The next day, he asked for a five-story house. His house was transformed beautifully. But his neighbors now had ten-story mansions. His devotion was his, but the joy was theirs. His heart began to burn.

He went to a friend and asked, "What should I do? I want blessings, but I don't want my neighbors to be happier." The friend said, "Next time God appears, just ask for one thing: Ask Him to take away one of your eyes." God came again. The man asked for one eye to be removed. God granted the wish. The man lost one eye. And his neighbors lost both. At that moment, he finally felt peace. This is how jealousy slowly climbs up one more step and becomes malice.

Jealousy Is the Road to Malice

When you see someone possessing something you desired and failed to achieve, the sharp pain you feel is jealousy. But when that pain matures into a desire to harm them, that becomes malice.

Like in the story of Ansh. Ansh saw vacation photos of his colleague Mayank enjoying abroad. Mayank was glowing with happiness.

Meanwhile, Ansh was eating his regular lunch at his desk. Something inside him broke. He forgot that his own increment was lower because his performance last year had been weaker. Jealousy entered first. Then malice followed. He began criticizing Mayank, sabotaging him, and speaking ill of him behind his back. But life is fair in its own time.

That same year, Ansh's performance declined further. And eventually, he lost his job. But jealousy does not end with consequences. It repeats wherever the person goes, until understood and released. Because when your focus is on others, you lose focus on yourself.

Life is Not Meant for Malice

We have all seen people fall from great heights because of hatred. Malice never gives joy. It only brings defeat, loneliness, and loss. If you are unable to progress in life, ask yourself: Is my heart carrying jealousy? If yes, release it today. Celebrate others. Wish well to others. Life becomes lighter, clearer, and more beautiful.

Life is a Puppet of Emotions

Our body is like a puppet, and our emotions pull its strings: Joy, sorrow, fear, anger, love, compassion, shame, jealousy. These emotions make us dance in their rhythm. But among all of them, malice is the most destructive. Whatever we think and feel becomes the energy we send into the universe. And the universe always returns that energy to us.

Kabir Das Ji has already said:

> Kabira stood in the marketplace, wishing well for all. No friendship, no enmity, just prayers for everyone[2].

2 कबीरा खड़ा बाज़ार में, माँगे सबकी ख़ैर
ना काहू से दोस्ती, ना काहू से बैर।

When your heart is neutral, neither clinging nor hating then you become free.

End Jealousy, But Do It Quietly

In King Devaraj's kingdom lived Jaypal, a master sculptor. When he created a beautiful idol, the king rewarded him greatly. Other sculptors grew jealous and claimed flaws in the statue. The king asked Jaypal to correct the flaws. Jaypal understood the jealousy behind it, but he agreed.

For 15 days, he locked himself in a room, hammering and chiseling loudly every day. When the idol was brought out, it was the same—untouched, flawless. Jaypal said, "There was no flaw to correct. I simply chose peace over argument. I punished no one. I only chose silence." The king was moved. He appointed Jaypal as his royal sculptor. Jealousy dissolved. Not through revenge, but through stillness.

The Final Realization

Jealousy exists only because we do not know what we truly want in life. We chase others' lives without realizing our own path is unique. We were created by the One who created the universe itself. How can we worry about scarcity? Instead of **wanting more than others, desire the infinite.** Desire peace. When peace enters, jealousy and malice leave silently. Like smoke disappearing into the sky.

10

Willpower

Time never destroys dreams;
It is the desire slipping away that does.

There are countless powers in this world, but if you ask me which power I would choose, my answer is: Willpower. The world holds infinite strengths—knowledge, prosperity, courage, love, beauty—but none of these can succeed unless one essential condition is met: willpower. Willpower is the force that drives us toward our dreams and goals. It is an inner energy, a silent fire that gives us the strength to keep going even when life tests us.

When a person possesses willpower, they can attain any power they desire. **If someone awakens strong willpower within themselves, they become filled with confidence and courage.** Instead of fearing difficulties, they begin to view them as opportunities.

From Dashrath Manjhi breaking a mountain to Neeraj Chopra winning Olympic gold, the world is full of stories that prove that with strong willpower and unwavering determination, success can indeed be written. These people carved history with their dedication and commitment. But our biggest problem today is that we fail to choose the right inspiration and the right role models. We neither recognize true heroes nor walk on the path they show.

Take the story of Michael Phelps, the swimmer who won the most Olympic medals in history. His childhood was full of struggles and challenges. In kindergarten, his teachers told his mother, who was a teacher herself, "Your son will never be able to focus on anything." Young Phelps was mischievous and always wanted to be the center of attention. Once, in science class, he turned on all the natural gas burners just to annoy his classmates with the smell. In the school talent show, he wrote his name to perform tricks despite knowing nothing about them. He simply couldn't sit still. In his autobiography, "Beneath the Surface," he wrote, "It was difficult for me to focus on one thing at a time. I had to be in the middle of everything."

His mother encouraged him to try swimming because his older sisters were in the swim club. But Phelps hated water from day one. He wrote, "I hated swimming. I would scream, cry, throw my goggles, and walk out of the pool." But with time and practice, Phelps slowly began to feel at ease in the water. He began to channel his willpower in the right direction. He says, "When I learned how to swim, I felt a sense of freedom. In the water, my mind slowed down for the first time, and I felt in control."

His mother loved seeing him swim because she wanted his excessive energy to be used constructively. The three hours he spent in the pool brought him peace and balance. In sixth grade, Phelps was diagnosed with ADHD, but the pool became his sanctuary. At just 10 years old, Phelps became a national-level swimmer, and soon after, his talent paved the way to the Olympics. He went on to win a total of 28 Olympic medals, including 23 golds, making him the greatest Olympian in history.

In life, willpower is the strength that can turn the impossible into possible. No matter how difficult the challenges are, if we have determination and belief in ourselves, we can bring our dreams to life. Phelps not only conquered his fears and weaknesses but also proved to the world that with willpower, every obstacle can be overcome. In his own words, **"Where there is hard work and passion, there is no room for failure."**

Knowledge alone can leave any work incomplete. But willpower transforms that knowledge into reality. It gives a person the courage to materialize their dreams. It brings not only external success but inner satisfaction. Willpower is a fire that refuses to cool down before any challenge. It has the power to transform not just our outer world but also our inner being. As long as we have willpower, we can make the impossible possible.

Willpower is the truth of our soul. It continuously inspires us to move forward. It gives us the strength to rise above every situation instead of giving up. So if you ask me again which power I would choose, my answer will always remain: "Willpower." Because it is the greatest power of all. The one that opens the door to every other power.

Someone has said something remarkable:

> If your desires are firm, the scene will change.
>
> Otherwise dreams remain incomplete and lost in the fog.

Willpower and Nirvana

Prince Siddhartha, who later came to be known as Gautama Buddha, wandered for nearly six years in search of supreme knowledge. During this period, he sought guidance from the greatest sages, monks, yogis, and scholars of his time.

A famous story goes that his final teacher told him - "If you want to attain ultimate knowledge, gradually reduce your food intake. When you survive on just one grain of rice a day, enlightenment will come." Driven by a burning desire for knowledge, Siddhartha did exactly that. Through continuous austerity, he became so weak that his entire body turned into a skeleton.

One day, as he was trying to cross a flowing river, his frail body couldn't withstand the current and he began to drift away. With great struggle, he grabbed a rock and saved himself. Exhausted and defeated, he reached Bodh Gaya in present-day Bihar and sat under a Peepal tree.

At the same time, a woman named Sujata from a nearby village had recently given birth to a son. In joy, she had prepared a bowl of kheer as an offering for the village deity. When Sujata saw Siddhartha's weak, skeletal body, she felt deep compassion. She placed the bowl before him and said, "Just as my wish has been fulfilled, may yours be fulfilled too."

After eating the kheer, Siddhartha felt nourishment in his body and peace in his mind. Energy returned, and a powerful determination rose within him. He decided, "Whether I live or die, I will not rise from here until I attain enlightenment."

Then Siddhartha entered deep meditation beneath the Peepal tree. He remained in that state for six days and six nights. On the seventh morning, as the first ray of dawn appeared, enlightenment struck him in a single moment. This was the moment Siddhartha became the Buddha. The one who showed the path to Nirvana.

This story not only reflects the pinnacle of his willpower, but teaches us that **with unwavering determination and discipline, any goal can be achieved.**

Why Don't We Have Willpower?

Willpower is a mental and emotional strength that builds self-control and determination to achieve a goal. But some people struggle to develop it, and the reasons can be many:

1. **Lack of clear goals**:

   Without a clear purpose, willpower cannot grow.

2. **Lack of self-confidence:**

   When a person doesn't trust their own decisions, their willpower remains weak.

3. **Lack of discipline:**

   Willpower cannot thrive without discipline. Laziness and procrastination weaken it.

4. **Ignoring small wins:**

   People who don't acknowledge their small efforts lose the motivation to keep going.

5. **Fear of difficulties:**

   Some get scared of challenges and break down after small failures.

6. **Lack of inspiration:**

   Without inspiration, building willpower becomes difficult.

7. **Mental and physical fatigue:**

   Continuous stress and exhaustion drain willpower.

The inability to develop willpower depends on one's thoughts, habits, and mindset. To strengthen it, one must cultivate discipline, self-confidence, and positive thinking. Willpower is not an inborn trait; it grows with practice and the right attitude.

A Story of Willpower That Touched New Heights

This is the story of a man who wasn't born like most children. When he was born, instead of celebrating, his parents cried. This is the story of Nick Vujicic, who transformed his physical limitations into his greatest strength. Nick was born in 1982 in Melbourne, Australia, with a rare condition called Tetra-amelia syndrome, which left him without arms and legs. His parents, immigrants from Yugoslavia, struggled to accept this harsh reality. His mother initially refused to even look at him.

Nick's childhood was filled with challenges. Because of his condition, he was bullied in school. Children mocked him, laughed at him, and treated him cruelly. This heartlessness shattered him from within. He felt that he had become a burden on everyone. At one point, Nick even attempted to end his life. But in that dark moment, a voice inside whispered that ending life was not the solution. He realized he was alive for a purpose.

Nick decided to fully accept himself and turn his weakness into his greatest strength. He understood that his physical limitations could not stop him from fulfilling his dreams. He completed his studies and earned degrees in science, psychology, and social work. Later, he established himself as a motivational speaker and began addressing schools, colleges, churches, and corporations across the world.

One of his most powerful lines and my personal favourite is:

Believe me, losing hope is far worse than losing limbs.

Through hope and willpower, Nick not only overcame physical disability but created an identity that inspires millions. He participated in activities like surfing and scuba diving, proving that physical limitations are nothing but mental barriers.

Today, Nick Vujicic is a global symbol of inspiration. His story teaches us that with willpower and self-belief, any challenge can be overcome. Nick's life is proof that disabilities or difficulties cannot stop us unless we allow them to. His message resonates with everyone: **"Your willpower and self-belief are your greatest strengths. If you trust yourself, no obstacle can stop you from reaching your dreams."**

The Secret of Willpower

Once, a young man came to the great philosopher Socrates and asked, "Master, please tell me how I can strengthen my willpower?" Socrates listened and smiled. "I will give you the answer," he said, "but meet me tomorrow morning by the river." The young man arrived on time the next day. Socrates was already there. He asked the boy to walk into the river. The young man was confused but followed obediently.

As they walked deeper, the water rose from feet to knees, and eventually up to their necks. Suddenly, Socrates grabbed the young man's head and pushed it underwater.

Panicked, the young man struggled desperately. He tried to free himself, kicking and thrashing, but Socrates held him down. When he was moments away from losing consciousness, Socrates finally released him. Gasping and coughing, the young man inhaled deep breaths of air.

Socrates asked calmly, "When you were underwater, what did you want the most?" Without hesitation, the young man replied, "Air. I just wanted to breathe."

Socrates smiled and said, "That is the secret of willpower. When your desire for your goal becomes as intense as your need to breathe just now, your willpower will become unbreakable. When your determination becomes so strong that no obstacle can frighten you, you will make the impossible possible."

The young man understood. He realized that willpower becomes powerful only when we become fully committed to our goal.

How to Turn Willpower into Determination?

Willpower is a hidden strength within us, but to turn it into determination, it must be directed and strengthened. Transforming willpower into determination means focusing your energy on a goal and achieving it with unwavering resolve. But how does this transformation happen?

1. Set clear goals: Know exactly what you want. The first step to strengthening willpower is clarity. When your goal is clear, your energy and focus naturally move toward it. Vague desires never become determination.

2. Self-reflection: Ask yourself: What do I truly want? And why? When your "why" is strong, willpower automatically transforms into determination. It removes inner doubts.

3. Create a plan: Wishing alone isn't enough. You need a concrete plan. Break your plan into small steps so you can track progress and stay motivated.

4. Build consistency: Willpower strengthens with regular practice. Just as exercise builds muscles, consistent effort strengthens willpower. Take small commitments and develop the habit of completing them.

5. Find sources of inspiration: Read stories or watch videos of people who turned the impossible into the possible with willpower. These stories keep your motivation alive.

And remember, merely wishing does nothing. Every human constantly desires something every moment. But **not every desire becomes a reality, because not every desire finds strength.** Everything humanity has achieved was once just someone's desire - a desire that was transformed into determination. And that determination made the impossible possible.

11

Family

Ever since everyone got their own separate houses, the brothers who grew up playing together became guests in each other's lives.

You often hear people say, "You're like my family!!" Or, "This is a matter of home... you feel like home." But the irony is that many of these same people are living in situations where they themselves want to run away from their real home. They want to go far from their own family, and then somewhere outside, they begin calling strangers their "family".

But have you ever wondered, why does this desire even arise? Why do we start wanting to leave the very place where our childhood was spent... where every wall holds our memories... where every corner has seen our dreams grow?

The truth is, when we live inside our home, we stop noticing the warmth of relationships. We start taking our parents, our siblings, and other family members for granted. Their advice, their love, even their scolding begin to feel like a burden. We start believing that somewhere outside we will find more freedom, more understanding people. This is why the thought "I want to go far away from home" is becoming so common today.

On the other hand, when we actually move away from our family, that's when we realize that the belonging we were searching for outside... was always inside our own home. The same relationships we ran from were actually our biggest source of strength. The outside world may give you a momentary feeling of comfort, but it never lasts.

Today, people search for "family-like" connections in friends, colleagues, even strangers. "You're like my brother," "You're like my sister," such sentences have become normal. But can these really replace a family? Probably not. Because **family is that**

bond you're born with where blood connects you, where your emotions are understood without you saying anything.

So the real question is, 'why does this happen?' Why do the walls of our own home start feeling like a cage, while the outside world feels like freedom? Actually, at home, there are expectations attached to us. We're taught responsibility, care, and duty toward one another. And these expectations scare us. But outside, we don't owe anything to anyone. Yet the truth remains - the relationships you run from are the ones that give you real identity. They are the ones who love you unconditionally. When the world disappoints you, it is family who stands beside you to wipe your tears.

Thus if today your home feels suffocating, pause. Talk. Understand. Try to solve the issues. Instead of running away, try to understand your relationships more deeply. Because **outside you may find something "home-like," but not " home'.**

> Someone has beautifully said:
>
> Ever since everyone got their own separate houses, the brothers who grew up playing together became guests in each other's lives.

A Beautiful Story My Grandmother Used to Tell

Once there were two brothers connected by blood yet drifting apart with time. They lived in the same house but emotionally had become strangers. The elder brother lived on the ground floor, the younger on the first floor. The younger one had to use the outer staircase to reach his floor, which made him feel even more distant.

Whenever the elder brother said something simple like, "Tell your kids not to play late, the noise travels downstairs and we need to sleep," or "Move your car in the morning, I need to take mine out," the younger brother began feeling irritated, even resentful. He wondered: Why are we living like strangers in the same house? Why have such distances formed between us? Small things that once felt normal now hurt him.

Then one day, the festival of Holi arrived. Children from the colony came asking for donations. The elder brother, as usual, contributed. But when the kids took the outer stairs to go to the younger brother, the elder one suddenly shouted: "Hey! It's the same house, no need to go upstairs separately!" The younger brother overheard these words. And in that moment, something shifted inside him. It wasn't about the donation... It was about love. The elder brother, in that one shout, forgot every bitterness, every frustration... and said something profound without saying it directly: "We may live upstairs and downstairs, but we belong to one home. And our relationship is one."

This struck the younger brother deeply. He thought, "I began thinking of these as two separate homes... but my brother still considers it one. He still sees me as family."

From that day forward, he began noticing small things. He started thinking, "If my kids wake up early and make noise, I should make sure they sleep on time so they don't disturb others." He realized that elders don't complain out of selfishness... but out of concern for everyone.

Slowly, he let go of his anger. He began waking up early to move his car. He would stop the kids from shouting too late. He became thoughtful. Time taught him that distances in families are rarely due to big issues. They grow from small, ignored matters. And if handled with awareness, relationships automatically strengthen. Eventually, not just the home became one again... their hearts did too. This story isn't just about two brothers. It is the story of all of us. No matter what relationships we share, **if we pay attention to the little things and understand each other's emotions, no distance can survive.**

Small Things That Create Big Distances

Most household conflicts begin with tiny issues where ego grows bigger than the relationship. A small seed of disagreement, when watered by ego, grows into a huge tree - under whose shadow love suffocates. Salt was too much, someone didn't open the door on time, someone insisted too much on their own way, and so on. All these seem normal. But thoughts like "Why don't you ever listen to me?" or "Why am I always ignored?" add fuel to the fire.

Ego is poison. It turns sweetness into bitterness. When "I am right" and "You are wrong" become a habit, the walls of the house start echoing with tension. People start feeling like outsiders in their own home.

And you know what the worst part about ego is? It doesn't let you see who's actually wrong. Everyone feels justified. But this "I'm right in my place" mindset crushes others' emotions. If small disputes aren't addressed on time, they turn into deep wounds and love begins to die.

Therefore, before these small matters grow big, solve them. No one in a family is above another. **Relationships bloom only when we travel from "I" to "We."** When we begin understanding feelings instead of only winning arguments. That's when true peace enters a home.

Freedom - But at What Cost?

Yes, freedom is important. But abandoning family is not freedom. Those who leave their family often end up facing loneliness, insecurity, and a lack of stability.

Today, everyone wants unlimited freedom. Freedom from responsibility, freedom from emotional accountability. Family, which symbolizes love and safety, has begun to feel like a burden.

People are happy with "virtual connections" now. Instead of spending time with parents and siblings, they spend hours with unknown faces on screens. Depth in relationships is fading. People want instant comfort, even if it costs them long-lasting bonds.

Even if you achieve every dream, happiness becomes temporary when family isn't by your side. Success feels tasteless without them. Families stay strong only when everyone understands that nobody is bigger than the family itself. Living together, adjusting together, supporting one another, that is the real freedom, the real happiness.

Someone beautifully said:

> For the world you may be just a person, but
> for your family, you are the whole world.

The Story of a Little Girl Selling Watermelons

A small girl used to sell watermelons by the roadside. In the scorching heat, she worked all day to feed her family. One day, a car stopped near her. Inside were a couple and their little child. The child wanted a watermelon, so they asked for the price.

"Fifty rupees," she said.

The woman began bargaining: "Will you give it for forty?"

Meanwhile, the child insisted, "I want it now!"

The girl smiled, ran, picked up a watermelon, and placed it into the child's hands. The child couldn't hold it properly. It slipped, fell on the road, and burst. The child started crying loudly.

The mother snapped at the girl, "This is your fault! Why did you give it into his hands? Now I won't pay for it!"

The girl calmly replied, "I don't need the money. This child is like my younger brother."

She immediately brought another watermelon.

With love she said, "This one is from me for my little brother. I also had a younger brother once. But he got very sick, and we couldn't save him. So this child feels like my brother. One watermelon broke so what? Take this one."

The woman, who was bargaining a few minutes ago, stood speechless. Her eyes filled with tears. She tried giving the girl a hundred rupees. But the girl refused, saying, "Aunty, he is my brother. There is no bargaining in relationships."

This broke something inside the woman. She was on her way to a relative's wedding, carrying a gold chain as a gift. She took the chain from the gift box and gave it to the girl. "This is a gift for you from your little brother. Please don't refuse."

When they left, her husband asked, "A minute ago, you were bargaining for ten rupees, and now you gave her a gold chain?"

She replied, "Didn't you hear what she said? **There is no bargaining in relationships.**" Those words pierced his heart. He had been fighting with his own younger brother for years over property. They had stopped speaking.

He immediately called his brother and said, “Brother, the two houses father built, they were meant for both of us. I was the one stubbornly claiming both. Next week, I’ll come and transfer one house to your name.”

The younger brother cried and said, “I don’t want the house. I only want you.” The elder one said gently, “Little brother, relationships are never about bargaining.”

That small encounter healed years of bitterness. It reminded them that **true relationships are beyond calculation**. Life’s biggest gift is the love and togetherness of family.

How to Bring Peace Into the Family?

Maintaining peace and harmony in a family is essential. To avoid unnecessary conflicts and strengthen your home, here are a few suggestions:

1. **Value Communication:**

   Talk regularly. Give everyone a chance to express themselves. Solve problems calmly, not aggressively.

2. **Respect Feelings:**

   Acknowledge everyone’s emotions. Avoid dismissing or mocking anyone’s concerns.

3. **Let Go of Ego:**

   Focus on “we” instead of “me.” Don’t hesitate to say “sorry.”

4. **Make Collective Decisions:**

   Involve everyone in important family choices. Don't exclude anyone.

5. Control Anger:

   Calm down before reacting. Anger can deeply damage relationships.

6. Create a Positive Environment:

   Keep the home cheerful. Celebrate small moments.

7. Give Time:

   Spend time together. Understand each other's likes and dislikes.

8. Avoid Comparisons:

   Do not compare family members. Accept their strengths and weaknesses.

9. Don't Magnify Small Issues:

   Learn to ignore little things. Not every matter needs to become a fight.

10. Express Gratitude:

    Appreciate each other's efforts. A simple "thank you" strengthens bonds.

A family becomes strong when every member shows love, respect, and understanding. When everyone starts thinking about how to keep the family united, only then does a house truly become a home. And remember what I told you in the beginning. Outside, you may find something like home, but never "Home."

12

Ego

#Someone said something profound

When I think I've done something, ego appears;
when the world thinks so, respect follows.

There is a thin line between self-respect and ego. In self-respect, you honor yourself as well as others. But in ego, you want respect and praise only for yourself. Today we see many people who, after achieving a little success, develop a sense of arrogance in their behavior and that very nature someday drowns them. A person who walks forward with ego may progress materially, in wealth, status, and position, but when they look back, they find no one standing with them.

To escape this trap of ego, those who fill their behavior with gratitude and humility not only achieve success but also receive love and respect from the people around them. When you start shaping only your own sense of importance, you fall under the grip of ego. **You don't even realize when this disease of arrogance enters you, but it surely lands you in the ICU of failure.**

Once, I was travelling to Delhi on an early morning train. Winter had just begun. I bought a newspaper from an old man who sold newspapers at the station. He didn't take a single rupee extra, only the exact amount. He had a jute sack tied around his head. I went to talk to him and even tried to help him, but he politely said, "Beta, I don't need any help. If ever I really need something, I will definitely remember you."

He knew very well that we might never meet again. But the way he said, "I don't need help right now," showed one thing clearly that he believed in his hard work. **There are all kinds of people in this world, some full of self-respect, some full of ego. It depends entirely on you which category you want to belong to.**

During my struggling days, when I used to walk to the office, one of our seniors would cross the same road in his car. Since I didn't interact much with him, I never realized that he too took the same route. One day, he proudly mentioned, "This car... I bought it with my own hard work. I also used to walk to the office." Listening to this, I felt he was a hardworking and self-respecting man. But then he added, "Just the way he walks to the office every day, I also did the same."

I asked him, "How did you know that I walk every day?" He replied, "I see you every day while driving." And at that very moment, something inside me whispered that his self-respect has now turned into ego. He didn't realize it, but time had inflated his pride. Arrogance walks with us quietly; we don't notice it. When we drive the car, it's fine. But when the car starts driving us, the real problem begins. Then we stop seeing the people who walk on the road.

> Someone has said something truly remarkable:
>
> Ego comes when you think you've done something. Respect comes when the world feels you've done something.

My Grandmother's Wisdom

My grandmother used to say, "Beta, even the mighty King Ravana's ego couldn't survive. Then what value does our ego have?" Today, her words feel so accurate when I see someone's success collapsing under the earthquake of their own pride. Grandparents' tales hide the essence of life, but we forget them as we grow. My grandmother once told me a story that still comes to mind whenever even a drop of ego tries to rise within me.

The Sculptor Who Tried to Deceive Death

There was a sculptor in a village. He loved the art of sculpture deeply and spent his entire life carving idols. He became so skilled that every idol he made looked alive. People praised him endlessly. Gradually, this fame turned into arrogance, and he began to think that no sculptor in the world was greater than him. When old age wrapped around him and death neared, he began to think of ways to escape it. He wanted to hide from the eyes of the messengers of Yama (the God of Death).

Then he got an idea. Using his extraordinary skill, he carved ten statues that looked exactly like him, so perfect that no one could tell who the real sculptor was and who the statue was. His plan was simple: when Yama's messengers came, he would hide among the statues. The day came. Yama and his messengers arrived. The sculptor hid exactly as planned. Even Yama was astonished: "Who is real and who is a statue?" They looked at each other helplessly.

Then Yama smiled and said, "These are indeed extraordinary sculptures, but the sculptor made only one mistake. Had he not made this mistake, these sculptures would have been the greatest in the world." Before the messenger could respond, the sculptor hiding among the statues could not resist. His ego forced him to speak: "What mistake? There has never been a flaw in my statues!" Yama smiled and said, "There he is. Take him." The sculptor asked, "How did you recognize me?" Yama replied, "By your ego. Statues don't speak. Your arrogance exposed you. Your plan was brilliant, but your ego destroyed it." No matter who you are, ego always leads to destruction.

Ego Destroys Relationships First

Ego creates distances: "He didn't talk to me. So, why should I talk to him?" A person filled with ego loses qualities like patience and humility. We all meet such people - big positions, great lifestyle, but no friends, no real relationships. Once, they too laughed with friends, spent happy moments with family. But the arrogance that came with success took everything away from them. They smile in front of the world, but inside, they are deeply lonely.

Poor in Pocket, Rich in Heart

There are many people today who are poor in their pockets but rich in their hearts because of their humility. Even when their pockets are empty, when they see their loved ones smiling, they feel rich. And ironically, the person who abandoned all these people for the sake of ego despite having everything remains the poorest of all.

Socrates' Profound Lesson

In Athens, the great philosopher Socrates was teaching his students. A wealthy man came to meet him, but Socratesdidn't pay attention. The man grew angry and said, "Do you even know who I am?" Socrates calmly said, "Sit here and tell me who you are." Socrates gave him a map of the world and asked, "Show me where Athens is." The rich man pointed at a tiny dot, "This is Athens."

Socrates asked, "Now show me where your house is." The man replied, "Athens itself is just a dot, how can my house be shown on this map?" Socrates smiled, "If your house can't be seen on this map, then where are you in your big house? This is just one Earth. There are infinite Earths. Infinite Suns. Among all these, where exactly do you exist?" The man silently got up to leave.

Socrates stopped him and said, "Keep this map with you. Whenever arrogance rises in your heart, look at it. Your ego will vanish."

He concluded, "In this vast universe, we are nothing. Our false ego is the root of our suffering. The sooner we drop it, the better."

If Time Will Pass Anyway, What's the Point of Ego?

We all know this body is mortal. One day we must leave this world. So what is this arrogance about? No one knows what will happen tomorrow. But death is the only truth that is certain. If this body is to merge with dust one day, then where is the place for ego? Many times, we begin to think that we are the best. Loving yourself is good but thinking you alone are the best is dangerous.

Even the wise say, **Ego destroys all virtues.** With ego, we belittle others, often unintentionally insult them, and in that process damage our relationships.

> A Brilliant Reminder:
>
> Whenever arrogance fills your heart, take a walk to the cremation ground. People far greater than you lie there, reduced to ash.

"I Alone am the Greatest!" – Truth or Illusion?

I had a friend in school, excellent at studies, excellent at sports. Everyone admired him. Juniors saw him as an idol. But with time, ego entered his personality. It's true he was the best at that time, but he began to believe that he alone was superior. And that was the very moment he began losing his good friends. He remained at the top in studies and sports, but he lost every relationship. Today he has money, but not a single real friend.

Ego blinds you so much that you start hurting others. To maintain your false sense of superiority, you can cross any limit unaware of how much it is harming you. Whenever you feel "I am the greatest," look at someone better than you, your illusions will break instantly.

Why is Ego So Dangerous?

When we can't control our ego, all our virtues start fading away. People avoid egoistic individuals. Every society, every company, every home prefers someone who is humble, cheerful, and kind. **Ego is not a disease that spreads by touch. It is a human flaw that can be controlled with understanding and calmness.**

Change is the Law of the Universe

Life cannot become peaceful or joyful without change. Some people never escape their arrogance and because of it, they lose relationships, opportunities, and success. A person filled with ego believes no one is superior to them. The moment they feed this ego, they shut all doors of learning. They get trapped in the web of their own arrogance.

But if a person observes their relationships and stays connected to the people around them, they can save themselves from becoming arrogant. Remember— ego may give you temporary praise, but it earns you permanent dislike. People might respect an egoistic person to his face, but behind his back, no one likes him. A cheerful, grounded, and friendly person earns genuine respect everywhere. The choice is yours— who do you want to become?

Kabir Das Ji says —

In the end, this body will turn to dust,
then why wander in arrogance?
Kabir says, listen, O seeker,
the Divine is found in patience.[1]

We spend our lives being proud of our wealth and possessions. But this pride is useless - the body we boast about will one day perish. Everything we gather will stay behind. If the body itself is going to merge into dust - What is this pride about?

Kabir Das Ji further says that the divine is never found through ego. Only humility and contentment can lead you there.

He also beautifully said:

Water never stays at high places;
it settles only in the low.
Only the low can drink to their fill;
the high remain thirsty.

Ego is height. Knowledge is water. Just as water never stays at the top, knowledge never stays with a person filled with ego. To drink water, even birds must descend. **To receive knowledge, a human must bow down.**

---

1 आख़िर यह तन ख़ाक मिलेगा,
कहाँ फिरत मगरूरी में।
कहत कबीर सुनो भाई साधो,
साहिब मिले सबूरी में।

How to Destroy Ego?

In old movies, there used to be a villain who, after being beaten badly, pretended to be dead. And just when the hero walked away, the villain stood up and attacked again. Ego is exactly like that villain. It pretends to be gone but rises again. That's why it must be destroyed at the root. Three simple habits can help eliminate ego forever:

1. **Start appreciating others from today**: Say "Wow, what a nice shirt!" "You did that work brilliantly." "Your home looks beautiful." "You bought a new house? That's wonderful! So happy for you." Instead of noticing faults, start noticing goodness in others. Ego will slowly dissolve.

2. **Practice surrender: There is a devotional song:** "O Lord, if You look at my flaws... how will I ever cross this ocean of life?" The most beautiful emotion in devotion is surrender. Look within - You too have many flaws that you haven't been able to overcome despite numerous attempts. When you feel helpless, pray sincerely: "God, give me humility. Destroy my ego." Even the ego of Ravana had to be destroyed by the Divine Himself.

3. **Make small changes in your daily habits:** My neighbour, Mr. Agarwal, once gave me a wonderful suggestion: "Every morning, sweep the area outside your main door. It cleans the doorstep and also the pride gathered in the mind." I've seen many great people serve selflessly at religious places, forgetting their status and position, becoming just ordinary devotees. It reminds them that everyone is equal.

Always remember—**everything on this earth will someday be left behind on this very earth.**

13

Dreams

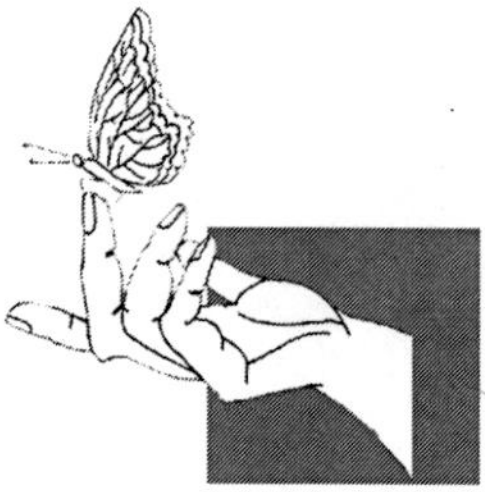

Dream high, Fly higher.
Because no matter what,
people will try to pull you down.

A human being spends one-third of life sleeping, and within that one-third, most of the time is spent in the world of dreams. Sometimes those dreams are beautiful, sometimes frightening. These are the dreams we see with closed eyes while we sleep. But there is another kind of dream, the one we see while we are fully awake. The dream that truly matters is the one seen with open eyes.

A waking dream asks something from us. For this dream, we must sacrifice our sleep. For this dream, we must keep moving. And perhaps, at times, we may even need to run. After giving up countless nights of sleep, when that dream finally comes true, only then do we experience a deep, peaceful rest, the kind of sleep that feels as if we have never slept like this before. Everyone dreams of a better life. But to turn dreams into reality, one needs determination, dedication, self-discipline, and consistency. Only with all these companions can a dream take the shape of truth. Always remember: the future belongs to those who believe in the beauty of their dreams.

Dreams must be seen, because when we dream, we move forward to fulfill them. But there is another truth: if we remain lost only in the world of dreams, we will fall behind. That is why, **once you have seen a beautiful dream for your tomorrow, you must begin working for it today, right now.**

I too once dreamed of becoming an RJ, an RJ who would not remain confined or limited, someone who would speak to people in cities, across the country, and around the world. Someone who would narrate stories, who would share a little of himself and listen to so much of the world in return. Today, I feel happy because I am living that very dream. This is why I credit my success to my dream. For if I had never dreamed, I would have wandered without direction. It was that dream which placed a goal in my life. And once the goal became clear, I could work toward it with effort and discipline, strengthening myself day by day. That is why I always say: Dream. Because it is the dream that reveals your life's purpose.

What Research Says About Dreams

The most significant research on dreams was conducted by Dr. Sigmund Freud. Through his studies, he explained that to understand the deeper layers of a person's mind, it is essential to understand their dreams. In his work The Interpretation of Dreams, he showed that even the dreams we consider meaningless actually carry symbolic meaning. According to him, dreams express our desires, either clearly or in disguise, desires that cannot be fulfilled in our waking life. For example, a child who wishes to buy sweets and toys but is afraid of his father's scolding suppresses his desire during the day, but the dream at night fulfills it.

As a person grows older, the fear of society becomes stronger. Because of this fear, one begins to hide improper desires not just from others, but even from oneself. Freud said that the human mind has three parts:

1. The Conscious Mind: This is the part where desires seek fulfilment through willpower. It connects us to the outside world.
2. The Unconscious Mind: This is the shelter of all suppressed desires - all those things we don't express.

3. The Subconscious Mind: This is where our moral self resides. Freud compared this to a state censor. Just as a censor filters news before broadcasting, the subconscious filters dreams before they reach our awareness.

Sometimes we see disturbing or immoral dreams and feel guilty afterward. To protect us from this self-condemnation, the "censor" reshapes and disguises the dream. And after waking up, the same censor helps us forget the parts that could trouble us - which is why we often don't remember entire dreams.

Why You Should Dream

1. **Dream it... to Ease Stress:** Dreams don't just shape your future, they also shape your mind and body. Professor Rosalind Cartwright showed through research that dreaming reduces stress. Dreams convert the thoughts in your mind into visual stories. When your thoughts are positive, those thoughts turn into pleasant scenes in your sleep, which keeps you happy. And when you're happy, stress naturally reduces.

2. **Dream it... to Make You Strong:** Dreams deeply affect emotional health too. Researcher Mokaimasín Den Boer studied Surinamese tribes and discovered that their ability to face hardships came from their dreams. When we face challenges in dreams, we become stronger in real life. Problems don't frighten us, we learn to stand firm.

3. **Dream it... to Give Life Meaning:** Life is given to everyone who arrives in this world. But a beautiful life belongs only to the one who has a vision for tomorrow - someone who wants to give meaning to their existence, who wants to honor the life gifted by the divine. All of this becomes possible only when you have a dream. A dream that gives direction to an otherwise directionless life. And that dream must be seen with open eyes.

14

The Ghost of thePast...

#Someone said something profound

We remember what should have been forgotten and that is why life stays tangled in conflict.

"Ghost", a word that can make even little children quiet and obedient out of fear. Isn't it strange? Since childhood, our family scares us with this word, and even when we grow up, this ghost still doesn't leave us. But now, the ghost isn't a creature in the dark. The "ghost" is our past. The past that walks with us, living in our minds. Those memories we should have forgotten yet cannot be forgotten no matter how hard we try. Think for a moment. Exactly one year ago, this very month, this very date, and around this same time, what were you doing? Even if you try really hard, you may not remember. Okay, try two years back, same date, same time, what were you doing then? Our memory is so weak that we can't even recall our "today" from a year ago. Some people can't even remember what happened on the same date a month back. But yes, if something unforgettable happened, you'll remember every detail: the day, the date, the moment. For example, I still remember the exact time, date, and every moment of my son's birth, because that day became a memory for life. Psychology also says this: Our mind remembers only what impacts us deeply. But if we stay stuck in the negative memories of our past, we will lose our path in the journey of life. So, forget the ghost and move forward.

Life is like the stock market—sometimes high, sometimes low, sometimes full of joy, sometimes full of sorrow, and sometimes filled with an unusual emptiness. We all know that good and bad times will come, yet we keep getting tangled in the bad memories. We stay stuck in resentment over something someone said long ago. There's a famous Arijit Singh song: "Man atak gaya hai, yeh man bhatak gaya hai..." Though written in a romantic tone, the truth is, this is what happens to us too. We get stuck in the past, and then we start drifting from our path.

Someone said something profound:

> All the things meant to be forgotten stay in our memories, and that is why life is full of conflicts.

One of my favorite stories is about Gautama Buddha and his two disciples. They lived in a monastery far away from the village. One of them was older and had been there for a long time; the other was a new young monk. Every day, both would walk to the village to ask for alms. One day, during the rainy season, they were returning when they came across a river, overflowing from the rain. As they were trying to cross it, they heard a girl calling for help. They turned around and saw a beautiful young woman. From her clothes, she looked like a royal princess. She greeted them and said: "I am the daughter of the king. I lost my way while hunting and now need to cross the river, but the rocks are too slippery." The monks saw that she needed help, but they also remembered their guru's instruction: "Do not touch a woman." Both were confused about what to do. Suddenly, the young monk lifted the girl onto his shoulder, carried her across the river, and set her down safely.

After that, both monks continued walking. The young monk walked peacefully. But the older monk was furious: "He has broken our discipline. He has brought disgrace." He walked at a distance, glaring at the young monk. After reaching the monastery, the elder monk ate angrily and decided to complain to Buddha. He went to Buddha and loudly narrated the whole incident. The other monks gathered too. Buddha asked that the young monk be called.

When the young monk arrived, Buddha asked, "Is what he's saying true? Did you touch a woman?" The young monk thought for a moment and replied, "Which woman? Oh, the one I carried across the river? I left her at the riverbank and came back to the monastery." He turned to the elder monk and said softly, "Forgive me, brother. You are older than me. But you are still carrying that woman on your shoulders." Buddha smiled gently and said, "If you remain stuck in the past, you can never move ahead in life. The young monk fulfilled his duty and then let the event go. But the one who didn't even touch the girl is still carrying her in his mind."

This simple story teaches us how essential it is to move beyond our past. Most of us suffer because we keep remembering old incidents. If we continue holding on to them, life will be ruined.

Forgive and Forget

The easiest and most powerful way to free yourself from your past is: forgiveness. Nothing good ever comes from staying trapped in the past. If we keep dwelling there, when will we work towards a better future? This ghost-like past wants exactly that: for you to never move ahead, that you stay stuck in its shadow. We must understand the past and not fear it. Learn from it, or forget it, and move on. Someone beautifully said: **"Never become a prisoner of your past. It was just a lesson, not a life sentence."**

The Weight of the Past

The past has no physical weight, yet it can feel heavy or light. Light are the incidents that happened but no longer matter. Heavy are the ones that still hurt, still haunt, and still trouble us within. This is where the "if only" begins: "If only I hadn't gone that day." "If only we had come back earlier." The weight is not of the incident; it is of the memories we refuse to let go. It is important to know what to preserve from the past and what to release.

A Story of Two Brothers

In a family, two brothers lived with great affection. They always shared everything. But one day, due to a misunderstanding, the younger brother spoke harsh words to the elder. Their relationship soured. A whole year passed and they didn't speak even once. When it was time for the younger brother's daughter's wedding, he thought, "Elders are elders," and went to apologize. He requested the elder brother to help in the wedding preparations.

But the elder brother refused. The younger brother felt hurt but didn't give up. A relative told him that the elder brother listened to a saint's discourses every day. The younger brother went to the saint and narrated everything with remorse. He requested the saint to convince the elder brother to attend the wedding.

The next day, when the elder brother came to the discourse, the saint asked, "Your niece's wedding is coming. What role are you taking up?"

The elder brother replied, "I'm not attending. Years ago my brother spoke such bitter words that they still sting my heart."

The saint said, "After the discourse, come meet me." When the elder brother went to him later, the saint asked, "What did I teach two days ago?"

The elder brother couldn't remember anything. He stood silent. The saint smiled and said, "You cannot remember the good things I said just two days ago. But the hurtful words your brother said years ago; those you remember word for word. If you cannot remember good teachings, how will you ever apply them in life? Better not come here unless you truly wish to change." This opened the elder brother's eyes. He realized how we hold bitterness in our hearts for years, letting it grow into hatred, yet we don't attempt to resolve it because our ego becomes bigger than our relationships. He apologized to the saint and then to his younger brother.

Those Who Forget the Past Build the Future

There are two words: Memory and Forgetfulness. Both are important. **Keep only the memories that bring you joy, that guide your path.** Look at the stories of successful people—their success was built not by remembering their hardships, but by forgetting them and moving past them. Some had broken families, some lost their parents, some had no money even for food, yet they didn't sit crying over the past. They kept building their future. A businessman once told me, "My family fought over our brand name. After years of court battles, I realized I must let go. I created a new brand and today that new brand is much bigger." Letting go created his success.

The Present Defeats the Past

If the past scares you or troubles you, remember you can defeat it. How? With your present. The best way to come into the present is: meditation. Some people practice it already. Some are trying. Some know its power but still haven't begun. Just 15 minutes a day can change your life. **You begin to realize how unnecessary it was to give the past so much time.**

A stand-up comedian once lifted a glass of water on stage and asked, "How heavy is this?" People replied, "200 grams, 250 grams." He then asked, "What if I hold it for an hour?" They said, "Your arm will hurt." "What if I hold it all day?" "Your arm may stop working. You might need a hospital."

"So what should I do?" he asked. Everyone replied, "Put the glass down."

Exactly. To come into the present, put the glass down.

Learn to Maintain Balance

I read the Yatharth Geeta every day, and I try to apply what I learn. Lord Krishna says: In happiness and sorrow, remain balanced. Our duty is only to make an honest effort, and the result is in God's hands. **Whatever happened was good. Whatever is happening is good. And whatever will happen shall also be good.** People who believe this live peacefully.

Don't Let the Past Become Your Present

This is the most important message of this chapter: Do not let the past become your present. What has happened should not happen again. Do not repeat the mistakes of your past. Otherwise, the past will return and become your present again. **Just as you stopped fearing ghosts as you grew up, stop fearing your past too.** Welcome your present with an open mind. Make it so beautiful that when you look back years later, you smile at the memories of today.

15

Destiny

#Someone said something profound

It is no accident that fingers reach
beyond the lines of the palm,
for even the One above has written
hard work above fate.

Whenever I hear the word "destiny," I start wondering, is everything already written? Or do we also get to write a little bit of our own story? I'm sure this question must bother you too. If everything is already written, then what can we really do? Can we erase what's written? Can we rewrite it?

In our school, we had a teacher whom every student adored. His way of teaching was beautiful. One day, he asked me, "Tell me, which animal runs the fastest?" I replied, "Cheetah." Then he asked, "Which animal is the tallest?" I said, "The giraffe, with the long neck." He then asked, "And which animal is the largest in size?" I answered, "The elephant." But his next question carried the real lesson. He asked, "Then tell me, who is the king of the jungle?" All the children answered together, "The lion!" The teacher smiled and said, "The lion is not the fastest. It is not the tallest. It is not even the largest. And yet, the lion rules the jungle. Why?" He continued, "There is only one reason: the lion's perspective. The lion sees himself as the king. His vision and his attitude is what makes him the ruler of the jungle."

"Destiny" is such a beautiful word. Some call it fate. Some call it luck. Some say, "My day was bad." And some say, "My time will come."

It was my first day of college. I was still trying to find which room my class was in when a sweet voice announced, "All BBA students, please go to the hall upstairs... your class is there."

I turned around, but she had already gone upstairs. Introductions began in the class, but my mind was only trying to find the name of that voice. And finally, the last introduction came, in that same beautiful voice. She said her name: Niyati: Destiny. And perhaps it was destiny itself that Niyati and I became friends.

Niyati was as wonderful a person as she was a friend. Helping everyone made her genuinely happy. She always used to say, "Whatever happens is what's already written."

She believed everything was predetermined. Like: "Nothing good can happen with my brother. His ways are just terrible." Her brother's name was Naitik: Ethical. Ironic, because he lived the exact opposite of what his name meant. Late-night parties, disrespectful behavior, careless attitude - this was his routine.

One day, I reached Niyati's house and sensed a tense atmosphere. I said, "I'll come later..." But her father said, "No, no, sit. You're Niyati's friend, you should know." And saying this, tears rolled down his eyes. "Niyati has cancer... and she has only a few days left." A few months later, Niyati left this world. Her words were right, everything is written. Maybe her departure was written too.

But then something happened that proved her belief wrong. The same brother about whom she said, "Nothing can change him." Her death shook him so deeply that he left every wrong habit and completely changed his life.

That evening, it was raining when he called me. His voice was trembling. "I topped the government exam."

I looked out of the window with moist eyes. It felt as if Niyati was smiling from above, and her tears of joy were falling like raindrops.

Two children of the same family, yet two different meanings. Destiny is written... and destiny changes too. This balance is the game of the One above.

Is everything really dependent on destiny? If destiny decides everything, then what is the role of effort? As a child, these questions kept circling my mind. But logical questions rarely get easy answers. We often hope for one thing, but something else happens. We call it fate. When something bad happens, we blame destiny. When someone succeeds, we credit destiny. Then what about the person's hard work?

My Guruji once cleared all my confusion. He said: "We read in scriptures that what is written will surely happen. But the truth is no one knows what is actually written. What if what's written is 'Only through effort will everything happen'? So, **when you don't know for sure, always choose effort.** Hard work always gives something - either success... or a new experience. So, when something bad happens, accept it as destiny, And then stand up again... to rewrite your destiny."

> Someone beautifully said –
>
> It is no accident that fingers reach beyond the lines of the palm,
>
> for even the One above has written hard work above fate[1].

---

1 यूँ ही नहीं होती हाथों में लकीरों से आगे उँगलियाँ,
ऊपर वाले ने भी क़िस्मत से ज़्यादा मेहनत को लिखा है।

Destiny – The Greatest Puzzle

"Maybe my business was not meant to succeed."

"Maybe this job was not meant for him."

"My luck did not favor me in the civil service exam."

These are sentences we hear all the time. Destiny... Fate... Luck. We remember these words only when we fail.

Friends, destiny is strange. Those who keep walking with full focus and effort. Destiny neither distracts them, nor scares them.But people who get stuck in excuses... Destiny becomes their shield to hide weaknesses. Now you might say "No one can control destiny, so how do we overcome it?"

You are right: no one can control destiny. But the key to this puzzle lies in two things within us, which we often ignore. The first key is intention i.e. our willpower, our motives. When intention is strong, obstacles fade and only the goal remains visible. And when a person sees only the goal, no power in the world can stop him.

But intention alone is not enough. To achieve big goals, we need the second key Principles.

Our values. Our ethics. To understand this second key, here is a story I heard from my revered Gurudev.

When Intention Shapes Destiny: A Story In an ancient kingdom, the king trusted his royal guru with his life. Every decision was taken with the guru's guidance. One day, the king showed the princess's horoscope to the guru. The moment he saw the chart, the guru was shocked. The princess had an extraordinary destiny — whoever married her would become the richest king in the world.

Greed took over the guru. He lied to the king, “Maharaj, the princess’s horoscope is extremely inauspicious. Her marriage will bring ruin. The only solution is to place her in a box and float it in the river. Whoever finds the box will decide her fate.” The king agreed. The princess was placed in a gold-filled box and set afloat.

Meanwhile, the guru ran to his hermitage near the river where he taught village children. He instructed them, “A box will come floating down the river. Bring it to my room. No matter what happens, do not open the door for me.” The children agreed. But destiny had other plans.

At the same time, a prince was hunting nearby. He had just captured a live bear. He saw the box and ordered his soldiers to bring it. When the box was opened, the prince saw a breathtakingly beautiful princess. She told him everything. The prince said, “Now what shall we do?”

The princess replied, “My father said whoever finds this box is everything for me now.”

The prince bowed his head and said, “As you command,” and they married right there in the forest.

The prince then removed everything from the box, placed the live bear inside, and let it float downstream again. Meanwhile, the guru’s students found the box, carried it to him, and locked him inside the room exactly as instructed. Thinking the princess was inside, the guru opened the box. Out came the furious bear. He screamed, but the children did not open the door, because he had told them not to.

In desperation, collapsing on the floor, the guru grabbed a piece of chalk and wrote on the board:

My wish is weak, God's will is strong. At the king's gate lies the princess, while the guru is eaten by the bear.

No story explains intention and destiny better. A simple tale teaching that intention shapes destiny.

Is Everything Written Already?

Scriptures say destiny can be changed through action. The Ramayana and the Gita both emphasize karma. Lord Ram could have destroyed Ravan instantly, but he chose preparation, effort, and strategy. Lord Krishna could have made the Pandavas win without war, but even they had to act. Destiny may write obstacles, but your actions decide whether you rise above them.

Destiny and the Mathematics of the Future

Destiny shows us a glimpse of the future, but the future is not what it appears. Picture this: a pregnant woman is sick. She dreams that her child will be strong, bright, and healthy. But if she ignores her present health, the child will be born weak. The child is tomorrow, but the mother's health today decides that tomorrow.

Another example: a drunk man speeds at 100 km/h and dies in an accident. People say, "This was his fate." But was it? Drinking and driving was his choice. He wrote his own destiny.

Life is a game of possibilities. Like cricket, losing the toss doesn't mean losing the match, and winning the toss doesn't mean winning the match.

Being born poor is not failure. Being born rich is not success. Success depends on how you play your innings. Opportunities come to everyone. Victory comes to those who recognize them and act at the right time. Hard work brings results only when it is done in the right direction, with the right strategy, at the right moment. **If you want to change your tomorrow, start fixing your today.**

Story of Two Brothers – The Real Truth of Destiny

I once heard a remarkable story of two brothers.

The elder brother attended spiritual discourses, practiced strong values, and lived a disciplined life. The younger brother, on the other hand, spent his days partying, wasting time, and believing that life was meant only for enjoyment. One evening, tragedy struck. The elder brother was hit by a car and lay bleeding on the road. The younger brother rushed him to the hospital, where he slowly began to recover.

During his recovery, the younger brother received a phone call that changed his mood instantly, he had won a lottery of ₹10 lakh. Bursting with excitement, he said, "You follow so many teachings and live such a disciplined life, yet you met with an accident. Look at me: I party, waste money, and I just won a lottery!" The elder brother smiled calmly and replied, "This is strange. We should check our horoscopes."

After being discharged, they visited a renowned astrologer. The astrologer examined the elder brother's chart and immediately pushed it aside.

"This man should have been dead by now," he said. "How is he still alive?" Then he looked at the younger brother's chart and exclaimed, "This man should be the Chief Minister by now! Arrange a meeting with him at once!"

Both brothers were stunned. “These horoscopes are ours,” they said. The astrologer asked about their lives. The elder brother explained that he lived righteously. The younger admitted that he simply enjoyed life and did nothing meaningful. The astrologer nodded and said, “The elder brother had death written in his fate, but his good deeds erased it. He lives because of his karma. The younger brother had greatness written in his fate, but his actions limited him. His destiny has now shrunk to merely winning ten lakh rupees.”

The story teaches one powerful truth: **Destiny may be written, but actions and thoughts can rewrite it.** Intention + Principles = Destiny. When intention and principles are right, destiny itself can be reshaped.

Can Destiny Ruin Your Life?

Destiny, often called fate or prarabdha, is believed to be the part of life that lies beyond our control.

But does destiny really have the power to ruin a life?

From a spiritual perspective, destiny is the result of past karma. In the Gita, Krishna clearly teaches:

focus on your actions, not on the results.

From a scientific standpoint, life largely follows the law of cause and effect. Those who blame destiny often do so to escape responsibility. Science tells us that **our habits, decisions, and consistency are what truly shape our lives.**

So no, destiny cannot ruin your life unless you allow it to.

History proves this. Personalities like A. P. J. Abdul Kalam, Rani Laxmibai, and Swami Vivekananda did not surrender to destiny, they rewrote it.

Destiny may hand you a set of cards, but how you play them is your free will.

So do not accept defeat by calling it destiny.

Rise with intention.

Act with courage.

And write your own story.

16

Enough

#Someone said something profound

We complain about having too little,
forgetting how many never reached this far.

From childhood till now, I have often heard my elders say: "Be happy with what you have." And, in my childhood, I used to argue with them: "If we stay happy with what we already have, then how will we ever move forward in life?".

Perhaps, back then, I could not understand the depth of what they meant. What they were really trying to say was: Learn to stay content with what God has given you. Because when you step out and look around, you realize there are many people who don't even have what you have. And there are others who have far more wealth, fame, status than you, Yet they are unhappy. Because they never learned to be happy with what they already have. So, they kept running and running, endlessly chasing more. In that chase, they didn't gain much. Instead, they lost the peace of their lives and lost those precious little moments where happiness could have been celebrated.

When I grew a little older, and my understanding widened, I realized: At the heart of what the elders were saying was one simple truth. The most important thing in life is to be happy. And happiness only comes when there is contentment. Working towards goals is necessary. Running with time is necessary. But celebrating what you have right now is equally necessary, because the moment never returns.

They say, **learning to be happy with what you have is an art. And the one who has learned this art stays far away from sadness, negativity, and unrest.** So yes, move forward in life, but remain happy with what life has already given you.

The Truth: Happiness Does Not Survive in Scarcity

We cannot deny this — if our basic needs are not being met, it becomes very difficult to find satisfaction in what we have. To live every day in financial struggle, to worry constantly about tomorrow, under such conditions, no philosophy works. Because every person, and every family, has different circumstances. So fight your battles according to your situation. Do not lose. If you persist, you will gain a lot in life. And then, that which you gain will truly feel like enough.

Is What We Have Ever Truly Enough?

This question must have crossed your mind too: Is what I have really enough? There are two answers:

1. If you decide that what you have is enough, you may stop growing.

2. But if you decide that what you have is not enough, you may stop living in the present moment.

And I believe - if you truly want to live happily, the second answer is more important. Because growth matters, yes. But living in the moment matters even more. French writer André Gide said, **"Being happy is not only a human need; it is a moral responsibility. Our joy and sorrow spread to others. Therefore, it is our duty not to be unhappy ourselves and not to make others unhappy."** If you remain happy with a sense of contentment, the environment around you becomes happier too. Often, we stop living today for the sake of tomorrow. And in that process, we lose so much. Because money, or any expensive thing, can return, but time does not.

So yes, work hard for your goals, but also welcome, acknowledge, and celebrate what you have already achieved. The greatest success is to feel, “I have enough.” Be grateful to life for what you have received. But this does not mean you stop moving forward. It simply means that you try your best. If success comes - wonderful. If success delays - do not lose yourself in sadness. That ability to stay steady, that is real contentment. And if you are content with what you have already earned, You are already truly successful.

Live in the Present - Be Happy Today

There are countless people who lose their present worrying about the future. Even if they eventually reach their goal, They often realize they have lost a thousand moments of joy along the way. So yes, plan for the future - but do not turn planning into worrying. **Work with joy today, and you will shape better tomorrow.**

Value People, and Happiness Will Naturally Come

Many people measure success through money and property. But my experience says, the people you win in life are far more valuable than the money you earn. Their love, blessings, and presence become your strength in your toughest battles. **Money alone cannot give that peace which even one genuine relationship can give.**

The Mindset of “Enough” Protects You from Greed

“More... and more... and more...” This hunger can snatch away the joy of the present moment. It increases stress and blinds us to all the good that already surrounds us. If you stay content with what you have, you naturally stay away from greed and wherever greed ends, peace begins.

Be Content, Yet Keep Working on Yourself

Thoughts like: "He has a car but I only have a bike." "My friend bought a house, and I'm still renting." Such thoughts neither help you move forward nor allow you to be happy today. There are countless people in this world who don't even have what you currently have. So instead of comparing, work on your own growth.

A Tibetan Story

In the mountains of Tibet, there was a lake surrounded by trees. It was believed to have miraculous powers: If an animal jumped in, it would emerge as a human. If a human jumped in, they would emerge as a deity. Very few people knew about this lake. And even fewer ever found it, because the path to it was very difficult.

One day, a wise man found the lake. He jumped in, and came out as a deity. A pair of monkeys sitting on a tree saw all of this. They said, "We have lived here all our lives and never knew this! Let's jump in too." They leaped in. They came out as humans.

The female monkey said, "This is enough. We have received more than we ever imagined." But the male monkey said, "No, I want more. I want to jump again and become a god!" She reminded him: "Our elders said, excess of anything destroys. Let's remain happy with what we have."

But the male monkey didn't listen. He jumped again, and came out as a monkey again. Because the lake had one rule: Transformation happens only once. The second jump returns you to your original form. The monkey, now angry, began leaping through the forest and ended up being caught by a street performer.

Meanwhile, the female, now a beautiful lady married a king. One day, the performer brought the monkey to the royal court to perform. The monkey saw the queen and recognized her. She recognized him too. The queen sent out a message to be spoken aloud: "Never be greedy for more. Learn to be happy with what you have."

The essence of this story is simple: Desires are important. Dreams are important. Growth is important. But at some point, you must say to life - What I have... is enough. And I am grateful. My grandfather used to say: "However long you live, live with a smile." Even today, I walk forward in life holding on to that mantra.

Someone said beautifully:

To stay happy in life is the real happiness.

I once heard Nobel Prize winner and author of the book, Thinking Fast and Slow, Daniel Kahneman, say "Happiness simply means being happy. We feel it instantly, in the moment."

According to a research, there are five things that can bring about a change in your life:

1. **Good friends and good relationships:**

   Having close friends increases life satisfaction by nearly 20%. A best friend can increase optimism and happiness even more. Being close to your neighbors reduces loneliness by 25% and increases happiness by 16%.

2. **Treat your life as a story and write it:**

   Those who write about their life experiences are about 10–17% happier than those who don't.

3. **Have goals:**

   People who have goals are 20% more satisfied with life. Small, consistent achievements bring more happiness than rare, big achievements.

4. **Not every question in life has "money" as the answer:**

   Those who understand life's meaning are twice as satisfied as those who only chase money.

5. **Keep learning:**

   People who continue learning throughout life feel more fulfilled and more meaningful in their existence.

But remember, no matter how much you achieve, do not lose your values. Pass them on to the next generation. That is where the deepest contentment lives. That is where enough becomes beautiful.

17

Gratitude

#Someone said something profound

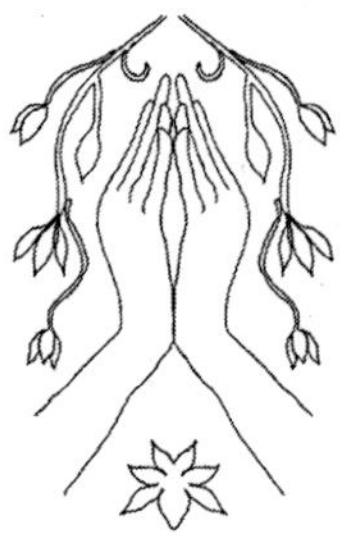

Everyone contributes
something to our lives;
no matter how great the ocean is,
it still borrows its water from rivers.

Gratitude is the most beautiful word in this world, because hidden within it is not only the joy of others but our own happiness too.

To feel gratitude for someone, to be thankful, to acknowledge the good — this is among the most beautiful emotions we humans are capable of. And the one who nurtures this beauty stays happy for life. Yet, when it comes to expressing gratitude, many of us hesitate. Some of us feel, "Why say thank you? Especially to our own people. Isn't it too formal?" I too lived in this misconception during my childhood. But the day I started saying thank you, even for the smallest help, something shifted inside me. I realized that the joy wasn't only for the one receiving gratitude. It was also for me, the one giving it. From that day onwards, I welcomed gratitude into my life. And now I say to everyone, whenever you get a chance, say thank you. If you still feel that saying thank you sounds too formal, then express it in another way. Make them feel special. Because when you make someone feel special, the happiness that returns to you is even greater.

Since childhood, my parents taught me: "The moment you wake up, thank the One above for giving you a new day." But back then, I always wondered what's the big deal? If night comes, morning will come anyway. It's automatic. But growing up teaches us the truth: the cycle of life and death does not follow our assumptions. Every night we sleep, there is no guarantee that we will see the next dawn. For many, a night can be the final one. It may sound gloomy, but it is reality. Every breath we are receiving right now is not something we are entitled to - it is a blessing. Just as my parents taught me, perhaps your elders also told you the same; **when you wake up each morning, say thank you to the Almighty. "You have given me one more day. One more chance to make my life more meaningful, more beautiful than yesterday."**

What the World Really Needs is Better Human Beings

Call it gratitude, thankfulness, shukriya, or aabhar: whatever the language, this emotion has the power to shape us into better human beings. It may not be possible for everyone in the world to become successful, but it is possible for everyone to become good. And so, why not walk towards what is possible?

In my view, this world needs fewer "successful" people and more people with beautiful hearts. And if you are someone who appreciates even the smallest gestures done for you, you are already on the path of becoming a better human being. Walk on it - it is a peaceful road. The more you walk, the richer your inner world becomes.

Shakespeare once said: "More important than an expensive gift is the respect for the one receiving it." This means that what matters more than what we give is how we value the person we give it to. And the first step toward respect is gratitude. Yet many people do not know how to be grateful. They believe they deserve what they got, so why be grateful? Some are always longing for "more." But gratitude means understanding that what we have is enough; it is precious and from this very place, more goodness flows into life. When you express gratitude, you do not become smaller. You become stronger.

Psychologists who study human personality have also found that expressing gratitude doesn't only make the other person feel valued; it makes us feel better too. This feeling strengthens the morale with which we move towards our goals. Gratitude not only elevates how others see us, but it also elevates how we see ourselves.

A story comes to my mind whenever I speak of gratitude: A bus full of pilgrims was returning after holy darshan. Suddenly the weather changed, with strong winds, heavy rain, and lightning. A bolt of lightning struck dangerously close to the bus. Everyone panicked. Someone in the bus said, "Perhaps our sins are not yet washed away, death is close."

The driver stopped the bus and said: "You may be right that someone among us still carries sins. And perhaps their death is destined today. So why should the rest risk their lives for one?" He suggested everyone walk one by one to a nearby tree, touch it, and come back. "The one who is destined to die would be struck by lightning during the walk.", he added.

Everyone agreed. People went one by one, each returned safely. Finally, the last person left was an elderly woman. Everyone assumed she must be the one whose sins were yet to be washed away. She slowly stepped off the bus, took the name of God, walked to the tree, and touched it. Lightning struck again but this time it struck the bus, not the woman. Because of her, all were safe until she stepped outside.

This is our life today. We assume others are the reason for danger, sorrow, and misfortune. **We forget that sometimes our blessings come from those very people whose worth we fail to see.** Stop looking at others with suspicion. Start offering gratitude for the invisible goodness they bring into your life. The moment your perspective changes, you begin to transform from within. Your soul purifies. Your thoughts soften. Your heart opens up.

Gratitude Strengthens Relationships

When we express gratitude, we acknowledge the importance of our relationships. **A small word of appreciation can deepen bonds in ways grand gestures never can.** Don't measure the other person's status, age, or role. If someone helped you even in the smallest way, thank them. In doing so, you honor them. And in their eyes, your value also rises.

Gratitude brings gentleness into our nature. It softens the roughness of ego. It reminds us how much we depend on love.

Where There is Gratitude, There is Humility

Gratitude naturally gives birth to humility and humility is one of the greatest virtues of humanity. Where there is no humility, there can be no patience. We seek humility and gratitude in others but how beautiful would life be if we first chose to cultivate them within ourselves?

Even Lord Rama walked his life with deep gratitude and humility, not only towards humans, but towards every living being. Without gratitude, love cannot exist. And without love, no relationship can ever be real. Humility means being willing to learn, to understand, and to grow.

The Greatest People Knew the Power of Gratitude

There is a saying: "Gratitude preserves friendships and creates new ones." The greatest philosophers have spoken of gratitude. Nietzsche said, **"The essence of all beautiful art is gratitude."** Steve Maraboli said, **"Gratitude is nourishment for living relationships."** Cicero said, **"Gratitude is not only the greatest**

virtue, but the parent of all others." And Jacques Maritain said, **"Gratitude is the most refined form of courtesy."**

Many people proudly say, "I am self-made." But they forget the fingers that held them when they were learning to walk, the grandmother's stories that shaped their morals, the teachers who taught them how to read and speak, the friends who stood by them during their darkest days. There are countless people we never thanked.

So today, let us put aside all pride and ego, and say: Thank You. Because now we have understood that Being grateful is one of the most beautiful ways to live.

18

Awareness

#Someone said something profound

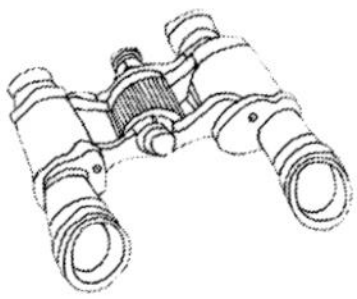

The world rushes ahead in unawareness,
while the awakened have mastered the art of stillness.

Call it awareness or consciousness; its simplest meaning is wakefulness — to feel what is happening exactly in the moment it is happening, to stay present in that moment. **Our consciousness directly affects our ability to act, and our success or failure is determined by the quality of those actions.** Which means that whether we succeed or fail in life depends on our consciousness, our awareness. If you are alive, then remain conscious too. This is the greatest proof that you are becoming a better human being. From a psychological perspective, consciousness is the element within humans that allows them to experience everything. Because of consciousness, we see, hear, understand, and contemplate various subjects. It is because of consciousness that we feel happiness and sorrow, good and bad, and it is through consciousness that we arrive at decisions.

In my school days, a teacher used to say something interesting. Whenever a student in class wasn't paying attention, or their mind was wandering somewhere outside the classroom, he would say, "You are quite the artist, aren't you?" One day, I finally asked him, "Sir, why do you call everyone an 'artist'?" He explained, "An artist is someone who is either acting out the events of a past that is already gone, or the events of a future that has not yet arrived. He is rarely in the present. He keeps roaming between yesterday and tomorrow. Similarly, when a student is not present in the moment, I scold them and call them an artist so that they return to today, return to a conscious state."

An artist's life revolves around recreating the emotions of the past or imagining the emotions of the future. But what compulsion do we have that we too remain lost only in the past or the future, and never arrive in the present? When in reality, we need to awaken our consciousness... live today fully so we can build a better tomorrow.

Even when we travel, our attention goes to clicking photos and posting them on social media just to show the world where we are. Because we are always thinking about the next moment. What will people say? Will they like this place that I visited? **Showing the world is fine, but first pause, breathe, and experience the place yourself.** Come back to awareness.

Doctors give anesthesia so the treatment can be done properly. But today many of us are living anesthetized lives, and the strange part is, we are not even getting treated. Instead, we are becoming more entangled. Frustration and stress follow us everywhere. We often ask questions to others, but sometimes we must ask ourselves too: Am I conscious? Am I really present in this moment where I physically am?

I have seen people travelling by train. Outside the window, you may see beautiful waterfalls along the hills but instead of enjoying the journey, they are busy arguing with co-passengers over something pointless. When they should be aware, appreciating the beauty of the moment, they lose themselves in unnecessary conflicts. A journey is supposed to help you untangle yourself from life's noise. But human nature often entangles itslef even more.

> Someone said a wonderful thing:
>
> No amount of wealth can buy back a moment that has already passed.

It is Necessary to Listen to Your Own Consciousness

A man once heard about a sage who lived in a small hut in the mountains, someone who knew the secret of the world's greatest treasure. The man travelled a long distance, met the sage, offered his gifts, and said, "Please don't talk in riddles. I want to get straight to the point. I've heard you know about the world's precious treasure, something that can make me the richest man alive." The sage said, "Wait for tomorrow morning. Come with me at sunrise."

The man did not sleep all night. He just waited eagerly for dawn. As the sun rose, the sage came out of his hut and took him along for a walk. The sage said, "You can create the world's greatest treasure yourself." "How?" the man asked. The sage pointed to a hill full of small stones and a nearby lake. "All these stones are cold. But among them lies one warm stone. The moment you touch it, you will feel the warmth. Keep that stone with you. Because that is the magical stone—anything you touch with it will turn into gold."

The sage added, "My guru once told me about this stone. He even demonstrated it — turning metal into gold — and then threw the warm stone back among the cold ones. I never used it, because my goal is not to become rich, but to unite my soul with the Divine." He then said, "Now I have given you the secret. You have the entire day. Find the warm stone and go home. Do not return to disturb me again."

The sage left. The man began searching through the stones. It was extremely difficult as there were countless stones. Then he found a clever method. He started throwing the cold stones into the lake one by one, thinking, "At least I can get rid of the cold stones. The warm stone will be easy to recognize." Hours passed. One cold stone after another. Finally, the warm stone appeared in his hand.

But he had practiced throwing stones for so long, for two straight hours, that before he could process the warmth and tell his mind to stop, he automatically threw the warm stone into the lake. Panicked, he ran to the sage's hut and cried, "I mistakenly threw it into the lake. What do I do now?" The sage said, "Do not even try to enter that lake. It is full of crocodiles. You will not survive." He added, "Your job was to keep the warm stone. But you were unconsciously lost in the habit of throwing stones. If you had been aware, today you would be the richest man on earth." **Whatever work we do, our mind must be present in that very moment, in that very action. Awakening consciousness is essential.**

Steve Jobs needs no introduction. Even his success carries the imprint of deep awareness. He said, "**Your time is limited, so don't waste it living someone else's life. Don't get trapped in a fixed mindset, living with the results of other people's thinking. And don't let the noise of others' opinions drown out your inner voice. Your intuition already knows who you truly want to become. Everything else is secondary."**

Had he not listened to the voice of his own consciousness, the world might not have known him today.

Consciousness Leads You from Outer Noise to Inner Peace

Many times we read a book and our eyes move across the words, but our mind understands nothing. We listen to a song, but we aren't paying attention to the lyrics. This only happens when we are not in a conscious state. If we observe carefully, most of our daily tasks are done in semi-consciousness. A perfect example is social media, where we scroll half-aware, not noticing how much time has passed, until suddenly we look at the clock. The greatest difference between humans and other living beings is that humans can choose their actions consciously. In scientific terms, consciousness is what keeps humans alive and gives them awareness of themselves and their environment.

Consciousness Teaches Us to Live in the Present

Bernard Haisch once said, "Consciousness creates reality." When your mind is awake, you live in the present and enjoy it. When consciousness is underdeveloped, a person either dwells on the past or constructs dreams of the future. To overcome this state, one must develop awareness.

The Sense of Right and Wrong

What is consciousness? In spiritual language, it is like a divine voice, like God speaking from within your soul. It helps you differentiate between right and wrong. In life, during difficult situations, it is consciousness that guides you toward the right decision. Just as we instantly withdraw our hand from something hot, or feel sad when someone says something hurtful, and these responses arise because of consciousness. When someone elevates their consciousness to the highest level, they begin to understand their true self.

Consciousness Shows the Path Inward

Osho said, "You may know the whole world, but if you don't know yourself, you know nothing." In philosophy, consciousness is considered a self-illuminating element. **Through consciousness, human beings expand their inner world and come to know themselves deeply.** Troubles are a part of everyone's life. No one is free from them. Problems will come and go but we must act with awareness during those difficult moments. If we master that difficult time, defeat becomes impossible. Our ancestors said, "All solutions lie within you. You only need to look inside."

Awareness Leads Us to the Soul and the Divine

Neuroscientists use the word consciousness to describe awareness. In spiritual philosophy, consciousness is considered synonymous with God. It is said that consciousness is present in every living and non-living thing and even in every atom. On the material plane, we gain worldly knowledge (Apara Vidya). But on the plane of consciousness, we gain knowledge of the soul and the Divine (Para Vidya).

Where scientists debate the exact location of consciousness in the brain, philosophers say every cell, every atom holds consciousness. The ancient sages achieved an extraordinary expansion of consciousness through purity and concentration of the mind. Their teachings guide us toward the direction in which human consciousness can evolve.

A Sufi mystic was once dining with devotees on the seventh floor of a building in Japan when an earthquake struck. Everyone panicked and ran. The host also ran but suddenly remembered the mystic. He looked back and saw him sitting peacefully, eyes closed, unmoved. Impressed by his calmness, the host decided, "Whatever happens to the mystic will happen to me," and stayed beside him.

The earthquake passed. The mystic opened his eyes. The host asked, "So much chaos. Everything shook. We all ran, but why didn't you?" The mystic smiled, "I also ran. The only difference is, you ran outward. I ran inward." He explained, "Out here, there was an earthquake. And where you were running, there was also an earthquake. Outside, there is only disturbance. But I ran to a place inside where no earthquake can ever reach. I sat there peacefully. So you see, we both ran, but in different directions."

Inside our mind lives an inner mind, an inner sanctuary. The outer mind gets entangled in worldly duties, struggles, and pains. But once we reach the inner mind, all suffering dissolves. **Reaching the inner-mind is liberation and this is moksha.** The mind tries to stop us from going inward. So we must discipline the mind through conscious awareness and wisdom. Happiness and sorrow are just dramas of the mind. The soul is always blissful.

When you connect your mind with the inner mind, praise or insult just stops affecting you, gain or loss doesn't disturb you, union or separation doesn't shake your peace. This state is called attaining supreme bliss, attaining God.

Awaken Your Consciousness

Every person has consciousness and must have it. I believe consciousness is what leads you to the door of success. And it is the expansion of consciousness that helps you remain there. Awaken your awareness. Use yoga, meditation, and pranayama. Read good literature. Engage in meaningful conversations with wise people.

The day you awaken your consciousness, you will shift from the "good" to the "extraordinary" category of human beings. In this fast-moving life, do not stay unconscious. Come into awareness. Live joyfully. Live healthily.

19

Spirituality

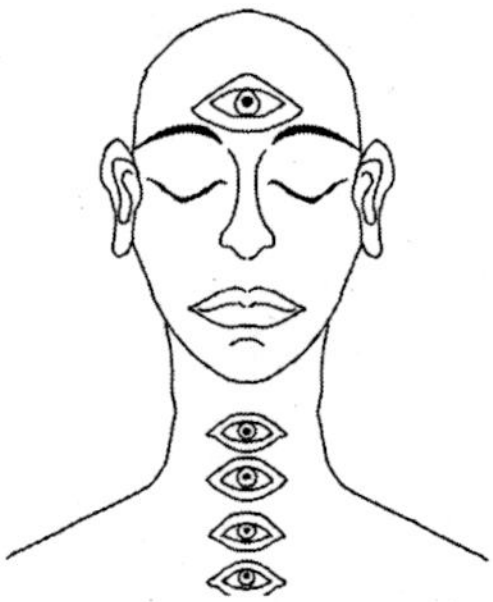

Spirituality begins where outer conditions lose the power to disturb inner joy.

Whenever I step out for the office in the morning, I always stop by Lord Mahadev's temple on the way and offer my respects. But for the last few days, roadwork had been underway, so I had to take a different route. It felt to me as if I was being denied the darshan of Mahadev.

It was winter then, and usually in this season, water tankers are rare. But that very day, a tanker came in front of my car, and painted on its back was an image of Lord Shiva. Even though I couldn't go to the temple, it felt as if Mahadev himself had come and given me his darshan.

That experience was very special for me. I realized that t**he Lord is everywhere; we only need to feel Him.**

Life places many kinds of milestones before us. Sometimes there is a rain of joy, and sometimes clouds of sorrow. Many people panic when troubles arrive. But **a person who has spirituality in their life cannot be prevented from living well under any circumstances.**

Early in my career, I kept myself confined to a narrow circle. I believed that what I was doing was the best. When I discovered spirituality, I stepped outside those boundaries. Spiritual experiences truly work; they give name and shape to your ordinary life.

Our sages have said, **"There is a power in spirituality that can turn a defeated life into victory."** You will have seen many well-educated people with vast wealth who nevertheless lack peace and contentment. The reason is that in chasing worldly possessions, they forget to prioritize themselves and their soul. So even when they have everything, there is unrest. The path of spirituality brings peace to such people.

From my small experiences in life, I have learned that no matter what the external circumstances are, if we remain happy and joyful from within, we are spiritual. **If we feel compassion and love for every living being, we are spiritual.** Spirituality does not happen somewhere outside; it occurs within us.

If we immerse ourselves completely in any activity, the spiritual process begins — whether it is studying, office work, running a business, or doing household chores. To know something deeply and lose yourself in it — that is spirituality. **For me, preparing my show is spirituality.** Bringing new stories for my listeners is spirituality. For you, doing the work your heart loves may be spirituality.

The root of our joys and sorrows is the mind. What the mind desires brings happiness; what it resists brings sorrow. Through spirituality, we can tame this mind and remain happy in every situation. In today's times, when mental illness is rapidly increasing, it becomes essential to include spirituality in our lives.

Why is Spirituality Necessary?

In modern times, why do we need spirituality? Why is it important to know ourselves? Before embracing spirituality, these questions naturally arise in everyone's mind — and rightly so. The need for spirituality is felt when we are not happy with ourselves or with the events in our life. In other words, when your inner desires are one thing, but life is showing something else. That is a state of mind where, even after having everything, you don't feel joy. And where there is no joy, whatever else happens makes no difference.

Someone once said a remarkable thing:

> Even if you acquire all the knowledge in the world but still do not know yourself, you remain ignorant.

Through spirituality, we realize that we are not this body but the soul. We are a part of God, who governs the entire universe, and if the whole is so powerful, then a part of it also carries that power to attain whatever we wish. Spirituality gives us patience and contentment, so that we are not shaken by any circumstance and can overcome it easily.

Wager and Peace

Two friends, Amit and Rohan, were arguing one day. Rohan said, "If a person has no mobile, TV, internet, or entertainment, they won't last long."

Amit replied, "No. A person needs only food, water, and peace of mind. Everything else is extra."

Their debate turned into a wager. Rohan said, "If you can stay locked in a house for one year without TV, phone, or any way to talk to anyone, I'll give you ten lakh rupees. But if you give up midway, you'll get nothing."Amit accepted.

Amit was placed in a closed house. He received food and water on time but was completely cut off from the world. At first, he managed well, but soon loneliness began to trouble him. Out of anger and frustration, he started kicking the walls. After some time, Amit realized that anger and restlessness would achieve nothing. He thought, "Why not use this time to look within and understand myself?" He then began to practice meditation.

Gradually, he experienced a strange peace and joy within. Days turned into months, and he lost all sense of time.

When only one day remained to complete the challenge, Amit pressed the gate button and decided to leave. He left behind a note that read:

"Friend, I do not want the ten lakh rupees. I have found a treasure within me that is priceless. That treasure is Supreme Peace."

Meanwhile, Rohan's situation had deteriorated. He had gone bankrupt and thought, "If Amit wins this bet, I'll have to pay ten lakh rupees. It would be better if I remove the button connection and keep him locked inside."

But when he reached the house, his eyes widened. The house was empty. Amit had already left, leaving only his note behind.

Rohan realized that **the true treasure is not material wealth but inner peace.** Even amid hardships, we can look within and experience true happiness.

Greed, anger, attachment, jealousy, ego — these are our greatest enemies, and today everyone struggles with them. These faults arise from the mind. That is why it is said that the one who conquers the mind conquers the world. To remove these faults from life, spirituality is essential.

A simple example makes this clear. Suppose a spiritual person's neighbor wins the lottery. The spiritual person remains unaffected and happy in his own life. Another person, however, becomes upset seeing his neighbor's prosperity. He becomes irritable, treats people poorly, and his friends distance themselves. This leads to mental distress. Then a friend suggests spiritual practice, and slowly he overcomes his troubles and begins to live better.

That is the glory of spirituality and its impact on our lives. Spirituality is the medicine that can treat every illness related to mental health.

> Someone wisely said:
>
> If there is a war in your mind, you need scripture, not weapons.
>
> The spiritual journey begins after knowing oneself

Swami Vivekananda says, "**No one can be your spiritual guru except your own soul.** You can understand what spirituality is from others, but the assistance in experiencing and knowing it can come only from yourself. After knowing the soul, your true self, you can walk the path of spirituality."

The first step of the spiritual journey is to know oneself; only after knowing yourself does the journey truly begin. **All activities that make us pure and lead us toward completeness are part of spirituality.**

For me, the spiritual journey is a personal experience that must be undertaken personally. Put simply, the spiritual journey is the inward journey from the outer world. It begins with the peace of our mind and the quieting of our thoughts.

Despite all the world's wealth and fame, without self-knowledge we remain like:

> Like the musk in the deer's navel, the deer searches for it in the forest.

This means there comes a time when the musk's fragrance emanates from the deer's navel, and the ignorant deer searches the whole forest for that scent. Similarly, the Divine resides within humans, yet humans seek it outside.

The King and the Treasure in the Cave

There was once a king who amassed great spoils and hid his treasure in a cave. The cave's entrance was sealed by a huge stone, and only the king and his close minister knew of its existence.

One day the king thought, "Let me see how large my treasure has become." He went to the forest cave. The minister was walking the same way and saw the cave door open. Fearful, he thought perhaps he had forgotten to close it earlier. In panic, the minister placed a heavy stone over the doorway and sealed the cave, not realizing that the king was still inside.

Inside the cave, the king was rejoicing at the sight of his treasure. When he tried to leave, he found the entrance sealed. He struggled desperately to move the stone, but it would not budge. Weakened by hunger and thirst, the king grew desperate. In his final moments, he broke a diamond from his ring and carved on the cave wall with his blood:

"All the diamonds and jewels for which I spent my life could not give me bread and water. I am dying of hunger and thirst."

A few days later, the minister realized his mistake and rushed to the cave, but it was too late. He found the king's body and the words on the wall. He understood that true wealth is not material.

The spiritual lesson is that the glitter of material things is fleeting. Money and treasure cannot give life's most essential needs: peace, contentment, and love. The king wasted his life chasing possessions, and only at the end did he realize that true wealth lies in inner peace and spirituality.

Alongside material things, spirituality is necessary in life. It teaches us that happiness and contentment do not come from outside but from within. When we look inside and recognize true happiness, we can remain balanced and calm in any circumstance.

How Can We Begin to Understand Spirituality?

Spirituality is not a complicated theory. It is a simple, natural process of life that anyone can understand and adopt. A common person can relate to it in daily life as follows:

1. **Recognize yourself** -

   The first step towards spirituality is knowing yourself. Reflect on questions like "Who am I?" and "Why am I here?" Understand your emotions, thoughts, and habits. Realize that you are not just body and mind, but that there is a calm, steady soul within you. A simple way: spend 5–10 minutes each day with yourself, considering what you did well today and what you could improve.

2. **Meditation and Pranayam** -

   Meditation and pranayam (breath control) are simple ways for a common person to access spirituality.

   - **Meditation:** Sit quietly with your eyes closed for a few minutes daily and focus on your breath.
   - **Pranayama:** Take deep, conscious breaths in and out. This calms the mind and clarifies thoughts.

3. **Adopt positive thinking** -

   Spirituality also means starting to view life with a positive outlook. Find joy in small things. Learn to forgive others' mistakes. Avoid negativity and think well. If a problem arises, ask yourself, "What can this teach me?"

4. **Help others -**

   Helping others or serving them is one of the easiest and most effective ways to practice spirituality. Assist the poor. Pray for the health and happiness of others. Support people in their difficulties. When you do good for another, you experience joy and peace within.

5. **Stay close to nature -**

   Begin your day with small habits like: Watching the sunrise. Enjoying trees, flowers, and birds. Spending some time under the open sky. This helps you feel connected to the vast creation.

6. **Practice gratitude -**

   Express gratitude for whatever you receive in daily life. Thank your health, family, work, and life. Remember that life is a gift.

Spirituality does not mean learning something new. It means realizing what is already within you - peace, love, and balance. The simplest way to understand spirituality is to live life with truth, compassion, and contentment.

The King and his Four Wives

Long ago, there was a king with four beautiful and virtuous wives. He loved each of them deeply, but the fourth wife was his favorite, followed by the third, second, and first. The first wife was the eldest and the least valued.

One day the king went hunting. A strange insect bit him, and he fell gravely ill. Many physicians and sorcerers tried their arts, but there was no improvement. Eventually, they said the king would die soon.

The king decided to divide his wealth among his queens, but instead of an equal distribution, he wanted to know who loved him most. He devised a clever plan and called each queen one by one.

He began with his fourth wife, his favorite. He told her, “I have only three days left. I want to give you an opportunity. Long ago, a sage gave me a powerful device that will grant me heaven, but for that we must go together. Before entering heaven, we will endure painful torment and spend seven years in hell. Since we love each other so much, will you come with me?”

The fourth wife responded without emotion, “My lord, I love you greatly, but I cherish this life. I would prefer to stay.”

The king was disappointed but did not give up. He called the third wife and asked the same question. She said, “I am proud of you and will prove my love, but I cannot leave my life behind.” By now, the king was very disheartened.

He asked his second wife, who had always stood by him. She said, “My lord, I would think of dying with you, but I cannot help you. I will stay with you until your farewell.”

Finally, it was the turn of the first wife — the one who had always been neglected because she was eldest and quiet. The king asked her the same question. She replied, “My lord, I will always be with you. Whether in life or death, I will walk with you.”

The king realized that his first wife alone was with him unconditionally. He felt remorse for having ignored her all this while. He apologized and understood that the most precious thing he had let go of was his character and values.

This story is not simply about a king and his wives; it is about you and me. Each of us has four "wives" in life:

- The fourth wife is our body - we adorn it, dress it in fine clothes and jewelry, but in the end it leaves us.
- The third wife is wealth and possessions - we spend a large part of life filling the home with goods, but possessions don't accompany us forever.
- The second wife is family and friends - they stand by us in joys and sorrows, but at most they may come to bid us goodbye; they cannot walk with us beyond a point.
- The first wife is our soul - we came with the soul and we will depart with the soul. We often neglect it, yet it is the one that never leaves us, even after death.

Most people live like the king in this story, loving their "wives" in the same order. **While it is necessary to live comfortably, care for family, and enjoy possessions, the true purpose of life is to pay attention to spiritual progress.**

Spiritual progress means understanding the deeper purpose of the soul, mind, and life, and developing inner peace and balance. It is a process of soul development, purifying the mind, and discovering the meaning of life. Spiritual advancement is a continuous journey through which a person recognizes and fully reveals the true nature hidden within. It is a journey to understand life's real purpose, cultivate inner peace and love, and become an inspiration for others.

Spiritual progress is the highest goal of life. I hope you will spend some time each day reading and reflecting on scriptures, and that by seeking the company of realized masters, you will feel spirituality more closely.

20

Meditation

In life, both prayer and meditation are essential: in prayer, we speak to God; in meditation, we listen.

When I was a child, my parents would always say one word before I began any task. That word was dhyaan, meaning attention. They would say, "Beta, if you are having breakfast, do it attentively. If you are studying, do it attentively." At that young age, hearing the same word again and again used to irritate me.

Then one day, my father explained the true meaning behind it. He said, "Look, beta, your mother and I repeatedly tell you to do everything with attention because it is extremely important for your life. When you do something with full attention, it gets done beautifully. Sometimes we understand the meaning of a word much later. But remember, only those who truly love you tell you to stay attentive. When you eat with attention, your health improves. When you study with attention, you learn more in less time. When you ride your bicycle with attention, you won't fall. This attention is what improves every action of your life."

You must have seen people who look at their phones or watch TV even while eating. They neither eat properly nor watch properly because their attention is nowhere. And perhaps, at times, you and I do the same.

Meditation is a mental process in which a person gathers their wandering mind, disconnects from the external world, and takes their consciousness into a higher state of awareness. It is considered a path to peace, balance, and calmness of the mind and soul. The literal meaning of dhyaan is "to hold" or "to stabilize the mind." It is a central part of yoga and spiritual practice.

The Simple Meaning of Meditation

Meditation is that state in which your mind remains rooted in the present moment — neither wandering in yesterday's worries nor entangled in tomorrow's plans. It is the process of lifting the soul to a higher plane of consciousness.

We climb up and down the stairs of our home even in the darkness of night without looking, and that happens with effortless ease. Yet, in bright daylight, threading a needle is difficult and requires attention. If attention becomes such an integral part of life that we can meditate effortlessly and carry out every action mindfully, what more could one ask for?

Everyone defines meditation in their own way. But for me, **meditation means becoming so deeply absorbed that you forget even the act of meditating.** It is like when you see a newborn baby for the first time — everyone becomes so lost in admiration that they simply stare. Or when devotion grows so deep that you keep gazing at the divine idol without distraction.

A Lesson from the Temple

There was a temple in my neighborhood where I used to go every evening. During the evening aarti, a large crowd would gather. One day, while I was sitting beside the priest discussing spirituality, an aunty walked up and complained, "No one comes here for devotion anymore. Everyone is gossiping with their friends, some are busy clicking photos, some are making videos. No one is actually praying."

The priest smiled and asked, "Aunty ji, what exactly do you want to say?"

She replied, "All these people are just doing drama. No one is truly devoted."

The priest said gently, "If you don't mind, may I give you a small suggestion?" Aunty nodded.

He continued, "Tomorrow, when you come, bring a small glass completely filled with water. And be careful — not a single drop should spill."

She agreed, "As you say, Pandit ji."

The next evening, as soon as she arrived, the priest said, "Please take five rounds of the temple with this glass of water, then come back."

She did as instructed. When she returned, the priest asked, "While doing the rounds, did you see anyone clicking photos? Anyone gossiping? Anyone recording videos?"

Aunty said, "No, Pandit ji. How could I? My full attention was on the glass so that not even one drop would spill."

The priest folded his hands and said, "That is exactly the point. If you focus on God, then who said what, who did what — everything disappears. Only the devotee and the Divine remain."

This story always reminds me that **whatever you do, become so deeply absorbed that only you and the action remain, and everything else fades away.**

Meditation means the quieting of thoughts, but thoughts will never fully end. So instead of saying 'the end of thoughts,' it is better to say that meditation means allowing only one thought to remain — the thought of the action you are doing in that moment. Different philosophers have expressed this same essence in different ways.

Every Moment Can Be Meditation

You must have heard terms like walking meditation and sleeping meditation. They simply mean living every moment attentively.

There was a boy in my class who used to get distracted so often that our Mathematics teacher would throw a piece of chalk at him at least three or four times a week, saying, "Where is your attention? Pay attention!" And he would always reply, "Sir, I was just watching the butterfly outside." We thought he was joking.

One day I asked him, "Why do you say such things? Why lie about a butterfly?"

He said, "I'm not lying. I am actually watching the butterfly. I find biology far more interesting than Mathematics."

Today, that same boy is a scientist in one of the biggest research institutions in the country. His story teaches the same lesson: your attention eventually shapes your destiny.

Life itself is a form of meditation. If you observe each breath carefully, you will realize that no meditation is greater than this. Each breath arrives after a gap and leaves without delay — a continuous, rhythmic reminder that meditation is life.

We simply forget the basics of life; otherwise, everything we need is always with us. This mind that gives us dreams also gives us the power to fulfill them.

Meditation Makes a Good Life Better

Doing every task attentively can make a good life great. But there is another form of attention that can transform your entire life, and that is meditation. In simple terms, **meditation is a mental**

exercise. One of its goals is to gain control over negative thoughts. It is said that for a fulfilling life, meditation is essential. If you want physical and mental well-being, meditate daily.

But a question arises: can this restless, powerful mind really be controlled? Once, a disciple asked Sage Vashistha the same question: "What is the most difficult task in the world?"

Sage Vashistha replied, "The most difficult task is to conquer your own mind." He said, "If someone says they have drunk all the oceans, I might believe it. If someone says they have eaten all the vegetation on earth, I might believe it. If someone says they have lifted the entire earth on their shoulders, I might believe it. But if someone says they have fully conquered their mind, I cannot believe that. Only a rare, deeply disciplined person can achieve it."

> Someone has beautifully said:
>
> In life, both prayer and meditation are essential: in prayer, we speak to God; in meditation, we listen.

How to Focus the Mind?

On Dussehra, I had the good fortune of visiting Paramhans Ashram in Faridabad and receiving the blessings of Guru Bhagwan Paramhans Swami Sri Adgadanand Ji Maharaj. In his discourse that day, he shared a story that answered many of my questions about meditation. I would like to share that story with you.

A merchant once traveled to another city for business. After finishing his work, he had a few hours left before his train, so someone suggested that he visit the local fair. At the fair, he saw a man with a strange-looking box. Curious, he asked what it was.

The man said, “There is a genie locked inside this box. It is miraculous. Whatever task you give it, it will do instantly. But there is one problem. Once it comes out of the lamp, it will not go back inside. You must keep giving it tasks continuously, or else it will devour you.”

The merchant laughed. “That’s not a problem. I have countless tasks to give.”

The man said, “If you’re so confident, take it. Give me five hundred rupees.”

The merchant agreed and brought the box home. Excited, he rubbed the lamp as soon as he arrived. The genie appeared. He began giving tasks one after another. The genie completed each task instantly. Within a few hours, all his tasks were finished. He even assigned work from the neighboring city, and the genie completed that too in minutes.

Soon, the merchant ran out of tasks. Fear crept in. The genie stood before him and said, “Master, what next?”

Panicked, the merchant rushed to his guru and narrated everything. The guru smiled and said, “This is very simple.”

At the merchant’s home, the guru instructed him, “Ask the genie to bring the longest bamboo pole.” The genie fetched it immediately. “Now tell him to plant it firmly in the courtyard.” Done. “Now tell him: climb up and come down this pole until I give you the next task.” The genie began climbing up and down endlessly.

The guru said, “My disciple, this genie is your mind. It keeps running, thinking, worrying, imagining day and night. If you do not give it the right work, it will devour your peace. Your breath is your bamboo pole. Make your mind climb up and down your breath. This is meditation."

Guru Bhagwan also said that day, "Meditation is very simple. When the breath comes, repeat a sacred name; when the breath goes, repeat the name again. Choose any short mantra you like: 'Om', 'Ram', 'Shiv'. Two or three syllables are enough. Meditation begins from here."

My suggestion is this: start meditating at home, and for deeper guidance, seek a true spiritual master who can show you the path.

After reading a book, listening to a sermon, or feeling inspired by someone, you may begin meditating. But after four or eight days, you may slip back into your old routine. My belief is this: **even if you meditate for just ten minutes a day, do it consistently**. With time, meditation becomes enjoyable. Once it becomes a habit, you begin to face life's challenges with greater positivity.

Call it meditation or mindfulness – either way, it holds a very special place in every life. It is the path to reaching oneself. Through this path, one discovers oneself first, and then the world. Meditation brings peace, joy, and meaning. Truly, if one wishes to find real purpose in life, meditation is a beautiful path.

Some people say meditation is only for the elderly. I believe it should begin in childhood or youth. Why wait for age to bring wisdom? The right way is to make meditation a part of life today, so that the coming years may be lived with zest and clarity.

Meditation: The Path to Happiness

India has always been the land of sages and seekers. Their guidance has preserved the essence of this country. Every spiritual tradition teaches meditation, because t**hrough meditation we discover who we truly are. To know oneself is to reach happiness.**

In my life, I have noticed that people who meditate usually live happier lives than those who do not. Meditation is known to increase creativity and positive emotions. Even a few minutes of daily meditation can make a significant difference. Research shows that meditation not only enhances happiness but also inspires people to do better in every moment of life. Studies also reveal that **meditation helps keep one youthful throughout life by eliminating stress and unnecessary worries.**

Today, most of us are tied to smartphones and gadgets. These tools, which were created for our use, now seem to be using us. That is why meditation becomes even more essential — to remain aware of how we use these devices. Otherwise, we might spend an entire day controlled by our phones without ever remembering to meditate.

The Five Reliefs of Meditation

1. **Relief From Stress:**

   Almost half the world struggles with stress. From children to adults, it has become common. Meditation is one of the most effective ways to reduce stress. It calms the mind and helps you stay stable and positive.

2. **Relief From Distraction:**

   Meditation sharpens focus. We often remain stuck in the past or worried about the future. Meditation helps us live in the present. Regular practice improves concentration, memory, and overall brain function.

3. **Relief From Insomnia:**

   Many people struggle to sleep. Meditation helps the mind relax, leading to deep, peaceful sleep. Good sleep improves your next day and your entire life.

4. **Relief From Illness:**

   Meditation and yoga help in reducing anxiety, stress, depression, high blood pressure, and many physical issues. Studies show it improves heart health and balances the body's energy.

5. **Relief From Problems:**

   Meditation boosts creativity and encourages fresh ideas. It helps you see solutions instead of getting stuck in problems. Life will keep bringing challenges, but meditation will help you handle them wisely and gracefully.

Just remember: Meditation will nurture your spiritual growth. It will lead you toward self-realization and inner peace.

21

The Gift

My Lord, what fear remains of drowning,
when the boat is Yours, the ocean is Yours,
and I, too, belong to You.

There is one thing that keeps us humans connected, no matter how old we become, and that is the joy of a gift. Even adults feel the same excitement as children when looking at a wrapped gift box: What's inside? What

We hold so much eagerness for gifts, yet we forget that one gift has been with us from the moment we were born. Let me ask you a simple question: what is the most beautiful gift of life?

If we ask different people, their answers will not be the same. Ask a spiritual person, and they will say God's blessings are the most beautiful gift. Ask a nature lover, and they will say rivers, mountains, and forests are life's finest gifts. Ask a loving couple, and they will say their partner is their greatest gift. Everyone has their own answer.

From a child to an elderly person, everyone loves gifts. I have never seen anyone who does not. Gifts bring joy, whether someone admits it or not. Whenever we receive a gift, we hold onto it carefully, protect it, and try to use it meaningfully. Even a small thing, a pen, a handkerchief, or a rose, becomes precious. That rose, kept inside an old book, remains there for years, and when the diary is opened, the dry rose and the memory appear together once again.

If we value these small gifts so much, if we celebrate them with such happiness, then why do we forget the most important gift of our life? **The most precious gift of our life is life itself.** Life is a sacred gift from the One above, and we should be grateful for it every moment.

This gift brings us the stories of our grandparents, the warmth of elders' smiles, the joy of speaking our first word, and the wonder of watching our own children grow. When we open this gift carefully, we realize it contains infinite possibilities in every moment.

Yet we often forget this. **This gift called life does not only give us existence; it teaches us through every moment, good and bad.** It gives us memories, lessons, and beloved people. It molds our identity and helps us understand the meaning of being alive. Life encourages us to use our abilities fully, to turn dreams into reality, and to move toward change and growth. For this, we must live with sincerity and a positive heart.

I once knew someone who was always unhappy with life. He constantly counted his sorrows. I knew him well, and I knew the real problem was not his life; it was his way of seeing life. Thankfully, he realized the value of life in time. Today, he is a happier person. Maybe someone around you is like him, or maybe that someone is you.

If yes, then today is the time to pause and reflect. Sit with yourself. Value this gift from the Creator, so that tomorrow you can welcome life with renewed strength and joy. Just as we try to keep a gift beautiful and safe, why do we forget to do the same with this gift called life?

Story of a King & His Minister

Once, a king was so angry with one of his ministers that he ordered the minister to be hanged at 6 p.m. that very evening. When the soldiers went to inform him, they found his house in celebration, for it was the minister's birthday. There was music, food, laughter, and joy.

The soldiers hesitated but eventually told him, "Today, at 6 p.m., you will be executed." Everyone froze in shock. The celebration stopped. But the minister said, "Thank the Creator that I have time until 6 p.m. Let us celebrate. Let us make this last birthday unforgettable."

People could not understand. But he convinced everyone, and the celebration began again. When the king heard of this, he went himself and asked, "Are you mad? You are going to die today, and you are celebrating?"

The minister bowed and said, "Your Majesty, you have given me time until 6 p.m. If you had not, how would I celebrate with my loved ones? Why should I waste the time I have? I want to spend every moment joyfully."

Hearing this, the king embraced him and said, "A person who values every moment of life deserves to live." And the minister's punishment was cancelled.

Living each moment to its fullest is the truest way to honor life's gift.

> Someone once said something beautiful:
>
> Life is not short. We are the ones who start living too late. And when the path finally becomes clear, it is already time to return.

Yes, it is true that sometimes life places us in difficult situations. We feel as if we have nothing. We think we are failing. We drown in negativity. And yet, we forget the most important truth: we have life. We carry a power that no other creation on this Earth possesses. We can think, feel, speak, love, dream, create, and imagine.

Stop criticizing the gift you have been given. **This gift brings joy, but it also brings challenges,** just as dusk follows dawn. When we focus on the positive moments, life expands. When we focus only on the negative, life begins to feel empty.

This reminds me of my childhood friend, Manish. He never appreciated any gift; he always found faults. So one year, on his birthday, nobody brought him a gift. He waited, and slowly his face fell. Finally, our class teacher told him the reason: "You never valued what others gave you."

Just as he was about to cry, I brought out the gift we had all bought together - his favorite bicycle. He broke down and said, "I am sorry. I always found faults in what you gave me. But today, when I received nothing, I understood the value of a gift."

Many of us are doing the same with life. We criticize it. We compare it with others. We see more ghee in someone else's plate, as the elders say. But pause for a moment and imagine: what if this gift were taken away?

So value it. Live it. Breathe in every moment. We have been given one precious life. Why waste it on small complaints? Be happy. Seek solutions. Cherish this invaluable gift. The way you repair and preserve other gifts, do the same with your life, because life itself is the most priceless gift you will ever receive.

This may be the last chapter of this small book, but consider it the first chapter of how you begin to live. Do not merely collect moments; live inside every moment.

This world, this sky, this nature, the rainbow after rain, the sun dipping behind mountains, the ocean glowing at dawn, the

music of rivers, the fragrance of the first rain - all of these are gifts too. We have simply forgotten to notice.

And remember, life is like a bicycle. It keeps moving as long as balance remains. I hope these twenty-one chapters help you build a beautiful life and inspire you to live in such a way that one day the world wants to live like you.